DEADLY

DADDY

Little Lost #3

Charity Parkerson

Punk & Sissy Publications

Copyright

—Warning: This book is intended for readers over the age of 18. Some of my books contain allusions to past abuse and trauma.

CHARITY PARKERSON

Editor: BZ Hercules & Consultants

Cover art: Temptation Creations

CONTENTS

Author Note

This series is a darker daddy/Little series. There's murder, suicide, and abuse along with heavy drug use. These are truly daddy/Little books with everything that entails. They won't be for everyone.

Introduction

Everyone thinks Banks is the carefree one. He's totally insane. That's exactly what Kyson needs.

Everyone fears Banks' older brother, Boone. As the youngest son of a crime boss, Banks tends to fly under the radar. No one sees him as anything other than a junkie. The truth is so much worse. Banks is the one who makes the family's problems disappear. His temper is terrifying. His conscience is nonexistent. The only thing that scares Banks is himself. Kyson is the only person who sees him to his core and wants him anyway.

After surviving unfathomable abuse from a man who claimed to love him, Kyson doesn't feel safe anywhere, except with Banks. He knows Banks is deadly. Kyson has seen him in action. That's exactly why he hopes Banks will choose to be his daddy. Kyson needs the protection, and the peace Banks' rage gives him.

Deadly Daddy is the third book in Charity Parkerson's Little Lost series where adorable, sometimes bratty, and scared Littles meet the men of their dreams.

CHAPTER ONE

WHEN LOOKING AT THE PlayPen from the outside, it appeared to be an uber exclusive country club for the wealthy. Only the patrons knew what really went on inside. From the swing sets to the rocking horses, coloring books and blocks. It was a haven for Littles. It was a hunting ground for daddies. No one knew that better than Kyson. Thankfully, Kyson also knew something even most members didn't about the place. A huge part of the building was a home. Inside lived

Kyson's hero—the owner of The PlayPen: Banks Bosi.

Kyson watched Banks circle the living room, eyeing his work. He had pitched a tent for Kyson, filled with sleeping bags and pillows. There was a flashlight inside, in case Kyson got scared. People were either terrified of Banks for his temper or steered clear due to his drug addiction... or both. As the youngest son of the biggest weapons dealer on the west coast, they were right to fear him. He was tall and skinny, but muscular. Kyson liked staring at the way his forearms flexed. Those arms had saved him. That was why Kyson wasn't afraid. The hands that had taken lives had beaten the man who hurt Kyson nearly to death. Then they had carried Kyson from the playroom to his home attached to the club. This was where Kyson had been ever since. Six months of healing. Quiet. The nightmares still came. Something inside him was still broken, but every day he saw Banks a little clearer. Each day, he wanted him a little more.

"There're coloring books, activity books, music, blocks, cars, and games. Oh, and snacks." Banks met his gaze. His dark brown eyes looked like home to Kyson. "Do you need anything else for your sleepover?"

Kyson tore his eyes away from Banks and inspected the fun zone he had set up for Kyson. His best friend, Soren, was staying the night. Banks had been so excited for Kyson; he had gone all out to make the night fun for them. He was the best daddy Kyson would never have. They were just friends. Kyson wasn't worthy of love.

"This looks amazing. Soren will have the best time."

A goofy smile touched Banks' lips. He could be so fun and kid-like when he was sober.

"Hopefully, you too. A sleepover is supposed to be a good time for everyone involved."

Kyson's gaze slid toward Shane. The lumberjack of a man leaned against the wall, watching. He was always watching. That was his job. Before Kyson had come along, he had been Banks' personal guard. Since Kyson's rescue, he had been assigned to stick by him. The poor guy.

When Kyson's gaze swung Shane's way, Shane smiled. "Don't worry about me."

"But you'll be here too." Kyson couldn't help but argue. For six months, he had been trapped with Kyson. No doubt the guy was bored off his ass. "Daddy—" Kyson froze for a second at his mistake and tried again. "Banks said everyone involved is supposed to have a good time."

"Give him some snacks," Banks said, heading for the door. He patted Shane's stomach as he passed. "Look at him. That's all it takes to keep him happy."

Shane rolled his eyes but smiled.

Banks grabbed his wallet and keys. "I've ordered pizza for you. It should be here soon. Also—"

Soren appeared with a different guard, cutting off Banks' speech. He was dressed like a fuzzy teddy bear and wore his backpack. As always, he was all sweet smiles and pretty eyes. Seriously, he had the most beautiful light green eyes Kyson had ever seen. He was so angelic-looking, with a round face and pouty lips. Not a single daddy ever looked his way because he was chubby. Kyson thought he was perfect.

He waved, looking excited. "Hi, Kyson."

From his spot on the living room floor, in the middle of the mess Banks had made for them, Kyson motioned for Soren to join him. "Come on. Look at what Banks set up for us."

Soren rushed forward, taking off his backpack as he neared. "This is awesome. I've always wanted to sleep in a tent, but I don't like sleeping outdoors. There are bears."

Kyson chuckled. "There's one here too."

Soren's gaze slid toward Shane.

A loud laugh burst from Kyson. "No, silly. You. You're wearing your bear pajamas."

Soren blushed, turning beet red.

Shane didn't help matters. His soft chuckle wasn't quite soft enough.

Kyson moved on. He knew too well what it was like to feel humiliated. "He's also got us a ton of snacks and ordered us pizza."

"Yay."

"You two have fun and behave." Banks' expression turned serious. "Brush your teeth before you fall asleep tonight. All this junk food will give you cavities."

They nodded. "Okay."

With their unison agreement, Banks nodded. "Good boys. I'm heading out so you two can have the run of the place."

"Okay."

At their unison agreement again, Banks tossed them a wink and headed out. Kyson didn't know if he planned to hang out just down the hall in the play area, or if he had sketchy shit to do for his dad. He never knew what Banks did when he left. Kyson told himself it was for the best he didn't know. It would likely break his heart.

Banks didn't know where he was headed for the night. All he knew was he couldn't stay. He desperately wanted Kyson to feel free. This was the first time since coming to live with Banks that Kyson asked if a friend could stay the night. Since Banks knew Kyson's ex-daddy had stripped him of every freedom, Banks needed Kyson to experience the night alone. Well, as alone as Banks could leave him with a gaggle of horny daddies running around inside the club. Plus, Kyson's ex, Jack, still ran around somewhere in the world. He limped now, though. An evil smile pulled at Banks' lips. He bet that motherfucker never forgot Banks, or the punishment for hurting a Little. Still, Banks wanted to clear out for the night and let

Kyson regain a piece of himself without fear of getting hurt for finding joy.

Banks cleared the hallway and stepped inside the playroom. He spotted his brother, Boone, pushing two Littles on the swings. His husband, Jupiter, and their lawyer's husband, Luca. The three were all smiles. God, it warmed his chest to see his brother happy and thriving. The guy fucking deserved it. His gaze skirted across the rest of the playroom. There were daddies playing cards and Littles all over the place. Banks' skin itched. There was nothing for him here. There never had been. Banks had built this place as a haven for others. There was no peace for him.

He kept moving, headed for the door. Banks nodded at the first guard he saw. "Has my car been brought around?"

"Yes, sir."

Banks stepped into the night air and found his Lambo waiting. The car had been a gift from his father. Boone had one too in a different color. Matching cars, ensuring both brothers always felt equally loved. Banks was torn about how he felt about his father. He loved him, of course. Growing up, he had been the greatest of dads. Then he had actually grown up, and the expectations began. Banks realized how many things about his childhood had been fucked up, and he saw how those things had led him into a world of pain. Now, Banks carried too many scars and emotions to live with them with a clear head. He needed to find Axton.

The moment Banks was on the road, he asked his phone to call the guy. As their attorney's younger brother, Axton had been on the fringes of their family for years. Except he spent those years behind bars for manslaughter. Since Banks arranged for his release, they had spent a lot of time together. The guy was fun. Trouble, but fun.

"Yo?"

Banks smiled at the way Axton answered the phone. "Hey. Are you getting into anything tonight?"

A low chuckle rumbled through the speakers of the car. "Always. I'm at the bar."

He didn't have to specify which bar. Axton only went to one. It was a shady biker place on the wrong side of town. Anyone else would be stupid to drive a quarter of a million-dollar car there, but Banks wasn't anyone. People knew him. They knew his father. That meant they understood they would never be seen again if they touched anything owned by him.

"I'm headed that way."

"Cool." Axton disconnected the call.

Banks shook his head. No manners. That was one thing Banks' entire family had in droves. They had grown up with the best of everything, living in two worlds: the highest of society and the lowest of scum. Banks could play either part. Oddly, though, Axton hadn't exactly been raised by paupers. His brother had become a well-respected attorney. Banks didn't know the story of how the two had turned out so differently from each other. Honestly, Banks didn't care enough to ask. He just wanted someone to get fucked up with him. Banks swallowed. Even losers liked company at the bottom.

Banks pulled into the gravel parking lot, maneuvering through the Harleys to find a spot to park. Neon lights and music filled the air, competing with the sounds of rowdy men and laughter. People looked his way and nodded as Banks headed inside. Banks didn't fit the scene. Everyone there was leather and bandannas. Tattoos and scars. Banks was clean shaven and polished. Jeans and a T-shirt that looked as expensive as they were. But these people still knew Banks was one of them. Just a wolf in different clothing.

He spotted Axton the moment he stepped through the door. His long, almost eerily platinum hair caught the light, looking like it nearly shimmered. The guy was hot. Chiseled face. Sky-blue eyes. A lip ring in the center of his bottom lip screamed he would do naughty things each time he smirked. Banks could see people falling at his feet.

Axton smiled when he caught sight of Banks. He stood. "There he is." He one-arm hugged Banks, slapping him across the back. "You should've let me know sooner you were hitting the town tonight. We could've made plans."

Banks grabbed a chair and sat. "I didn't plan on doing shit tonight." He started to explain about Kyson having a guest, but stopped himself. Kyson was good. Innocent and pure. He didn't belong in a place like this. Instead, he shrugged. "But I got bored. You know how it is."

A wicked-looking smile stretched Axton's lips. "You came to the right place."

Banks knew he had. That was why he was there, looking to drown his emotions. To forget. Maybe one day, it would kill him. That day couldn't come soon enough for Banks.

Despite having a great time, Kyson still split his attention between Soren and the clock. He never knew how long Banks would stay gone. Kyson lived in constant fear he wouldn't come back. Thankfully, they had run out of steam for playing games. Kyson turned out the lights and turned on the big screen. Side by side on their backs and on the floor, Soren and he watched an animated movie. It had been a fun night. It felt good to enjoy himself without worrying he would be punished for it.

Kyson hated that Jack still lived in the back of his head. He didn't love him or miss him. The love had been beaten from Kyson a year into the relationship. Fear had kept him from leaving. Jack had come too close to killing Kyson too many times for Kyson to think he had a single chance of leaving alive. Then Banks had taken one look at Kyson's bruises and turned into an avenging angel. Kyson had gotten used to violence. Yet he still had never seen the fury Banks unleashed that day. He had been like a berserker. Banks had been covered in Jack's blood when he had gently lifted Kyson from his seat and carried him here. He had inspected Kyson's injuries and swore to him no one would ever hurt him again. Banks had given him a home, safety, and peace. Unfortunately, Kyson didn't think Banks knew peace. Whatever Kyson had seen inside Banks that day, Kyson had a bad feeling that was the person Banks truly was, and Banks scared the fuck out of himself. Kyson wanted to save him.

The radio on Shane's belt chirped. He snagged it. "Yeah. What's up?"

"Banks is in his car out front."

At the crackled-sounding words, Shane's shoulders fell. He sat nearby on the loveseat, watching the movie with them. The defeat in his every line made Kyson's stomach hurt. Shane brought the radio to his mouth. "All right. I'm on my way." He stood. "Will you two be all right alone for a minute?"

Soren kicked one footsie-clad foot into the air. "I know Judo."

The way Shane laughed on the way to the door had the two exchanging a smile. Sometimes Kyson got the feeling Soren liked Shane. He was twice as funny in the guy's presence. Kyson wished he could push the two together.

All Kyson's humor died when Shane returned with Banks over his shoulder. It was obvious Banks was out cold. Kyson chewed his bottom lip as he watched Shane head down the hall to Banks' bedroom. In no time, he reappeared and reclaimed his spot on the loveseat like nothing happened.

Kyson rolled to his side and stared down the hallway. From his spot and angle on the floor, he could just see the corner of Banks' open bedroom door. His mind raced with excuses to go see for himself if Banks was alive. Then, like a zombie, Banks appeared in the doorway before turning left into the bathroom. The light flared to life, but the door didn't close. Kyson blinked. It was weird as hell. Banks had a bathroom inside his bedroom. Was he that out of his head? Was he sleepwalking? Kyson couldn't take it any longer.

He pressed his lips against Soren's ear. "I'm going to go check on Banks. Will you be okay?"

Soren turned his head and met Kyson's stare. "Of course. I'll distract Shane with snacks."

A chuckle burst from Kyson. The universe had opened up and given Soren a chance to be alone with Shane, and Kyson a chance to go be with Banks without guilt. He pushed to his knees and stood.

Soren sat up and focused on Shane. "Let's get some more of those cookies."

Kyson didn't wait around to see what happened. He headed straight for the bathroom. His heart traveled to his throat at the first sight of Banks. All his clothes were strewn around the room. He was on the floor, coated in sweat. His normally perfectly styled hair was plastered to his skin. Kyson stepped into the room and over his body, moving to his head. He dropped to his knees before finding a comfortable way to sit on the floor with his back against the wall. Kyson gently lifted Banks' head and slid beneath it so his head rested on Kyson's lap. He could see his chest moving, but he was scared Banks would puke and then choke to death on his own vomit.

Kyson felt numb as he stroked Banks' hair. He didn't understand why Banks always did this to himself. In every other way, Banks was perfect. He was beautiful and kind. He was funny and sweet. But then there was this scary side of him that needed Kyson to be the savior. He wouldn't leave Banks in his time of need. Just like Banks hadn't abandoned him when everyone else had.

Banks' eyes opened. An adorable smile touched his lips. "Hi."

Kyson smiled. "Hi."

"You look cute as hell as a Piglet. Did I tell you that earlier?"

Kyson's smile grew alongside the pains in his chest. Banks' eyes closed again and then reopened as if he fought to stay conscious. "I'm sorry I'm not a very good daddy."

Kyson's heart squeezed in his chest. He kissed Banks' forehead.

A sweet humming sound came from the back of Banks' throat. "Did you know? I used to have a daddy too."

Tears sprang to Kyson's eyes at the pain in Banks' voice. He swallowed past the lump in his throat. "I can't picture you as a Little."

"I was barely eighteen." Banks' eyes stayed closed, letting Kyson stare at him without shame. "He was like Jack, except worse. At least, I pray he was worse. I can't think about you going through half of what I did. My heart can't take it."

Kyson swiped his eyes. His heart was breaking. "What happened to him?"

"I killed him." The words came out in barely a whisper and Banks was gone again.

"Good." Kyson said the word under his breath, not wanting to wake Banks. He quietly cried, while still trying to keep Banks' head up. Kyson genuinely couldn't picture Banks as a Little. He was so amazing at being a daddy, but this was the first time he had called himself that with Kyson. Honestly, while Kyson sometimes slipped up and called Banks that, it was more like calling a man by the wrong name. He didn't expect Banks to take on that role. In fact, he didn't think he wanted another daddy. He just wanted to be himself in peace. In a lot of ways, he was scared to ever let anyone have that sort of power in his life again. He was scared of a lot of things.

"Goddamn it. You should've said something." Kyson startled at Shane's sudden arrival in the doorway. Shane stormed into the room and plucked Banks from the floor like he wasn't nude and weighed nothing.

Kyson scrambled after him. "It's fine. I want to take care of him."

Shane unceremoniously dumped Banks on his bed. Banks didn't move. He focused on Kyson. "If you want to love him, that's on your head." He pointed toward the bed. "But that's all you'll ever get."

Kyson fought another wave of tears. Not only from Shane's harsh words but also his mean tone and Kyson's humiliation. He lost the battle. The tears spilled over his lashes. For a moment, Shane stared at him, looking defeated. "Do what you want." He stepped around Kyson, leaving him to his overloaded emotions.

Soren wrapped his arm around Kyson and steered him from the room. He didn't head back to their tent and party. Instead, Soren led him to bed. He urged Kyson to sit before he climbed into bed next to him.

Kyson followed his lead and curled onto his side. He let Soren hold him.

"It's okay," Soren whispered, sounding exactly like the Little he was. "I know he's not without his vices, but I see you two. He's the perfect man for you. I see the way he looks at you. You're not wrong for caring. Don't let anyone make you feel wrong."

Kyson cried harder. He knew Soren cared and understood. But then again, no one did. No one knew the battle Kyson fought every day just to keep going. Banks gave him purpose. Shane thought he was stupid for it. What did that say about Kyson? Maybe he really was better off dead.

Chapter Two

THE COTTON MOUTH WAS always the worst. Banks would say it was the headache, but he never stayed totally clearheaded enough to be in pain. He woke up, lit a laced cigar, and then went in search of water. The place was quiet. The tent and fun zone he had created for Kyson were gone. All the furniture had been slid back into place. Banks checked the clock. It wasn't quite noon. Surely Soren and Kyson had already been up, and Soren had left.

The PlayPen wasn't open yet for the day. So, Shane was likely out doing his own thing. He didn't clock in until the club opened. Otherwise, Kyson was safely tucked away inside Banks' place. He padded his way into the kitchen. Kyson sat alone at the table, dressed like an adult, which never happened unless he had an appointment or something. Banks' gaze slid toward the calendar on the fridge. There was nothing marked for today.

"Hey. Did Soren leave already?"

Kyson looked up from his phone. His eyes were swollen. "Hey. Yeah. He had to work today."

Banks nodded and grabbed a bottle of water from the fridge. He plopped down at the table and chugged half the bottle.

Kyson went back to looking at his phone.

Something felt off, but Banks couldn't put his finger on it. Kyson never stayed glued to his phone. "Is everything okay?"

Kyson looked up again. His dark green eyes really looked puffy, and that bugged the shit out of Banks. "Yes. Are you okay?"

"Yeah." Even Banks heard the question in his voice—like he was unsure of his own answer. There was something wrong with his chest. He felt sad for some reason he couldn't explain. Banks needed Kyson to fix it. "What are you doing? You seem pretty intensely focused on your phone over there."

Kyson's ears turned red.

Banks had a bad feeling he was about to get angry.

"Um. I'm looking for a job."

Yep. He was angry. Banks took a drag from his cigar, hoping to temper his voice. "Why?

You don't need a job. Am I not taking good enough care of you?"

Kyson's gaze slid away.

Banks' heart dropped. "I'm not taking care of you." There was no missing the hurt in his voice.

Kyson immediately focused on him. "You take amazing care of me. I just thought maybe I should start looking for a way to get out of your hair. It's been six months, after all."

"Put your phone away. You're not going any-where. Nothing makes me happy except taking care of you." Banks swallowed. He sounded bossy—like an absurd lover. "It would break my heart if you left me. If you want to go, I won't stand in your way, but I'd miss you." Everyone left him. He shouldn't have expected more from Kyson.

Kyson set his phone aside. "Talk to me. What did you just think you don't want to share? I saw it in your eyes."

A sad smile pulled at Banks' lips. This was why he loved Kyson. Banks blinked at his thoughts. When had he fallen in love with Kyson? A vague memory surfaced. Kyson stroked his hair. He was only half conscious on the bathroom floor, but he remembered the sweet way Kyson kissed his forehead. Banks loved him. "You don't want to hear how ugly my thoughts can be."

"Yes, I do." Kyson set his elbow on the table and propped up his chin, as if settling in to hear whatever Banks had to say. "Just tell me that one thought."

A laugh rumbled from Banks. "Damn. You really want me exposing myself over here."

A gorgeous smile stretched Kyson's lips. "Just one confession. I'll even trade you. One exposing thought for one of mine."

Goddamn it. Banks really wanted Kyson to expose himself. "If I do this, you can't get mad at me or preachy. I know I'm fucked up."

Kyson drew a cross on his chest. "I swear."

Banks took another hit. "I thought everyone leaves me, so I guess I can't blame you for wanting to go."

"I don't want to go."

Fuck. Banks really hoped that wasn't his one confession. He wanted more. "Then why were you looking for a job? For real. Not just some bullshit about getting out of my hair."

Kyson blew out a sigh and sat back. "Last night."

"I'm sorry." The apology popped from him with zero hesitation. "You shouldn't have had to ever take care of me like that. I'm sorry I'm a mess."

Kyson shook his head. "It's not that." He blew out another tired-sounding breath like this conversation was pulling from his soul. "Shane carried you to bed and then kind of fussed at me. I don't know. Since I moved in, you've kept me so insulated, I haven't dealt with feeling humiliated in a while. It's not Shane's fault. I guess I just felt exposed, and I don't do well with people's anger anymore." He held Banks' stare. Then, unexpectedly, his shoulders squared. "No. You know what? I'm mad. I don't care what made you do what you did, but I shouldn't be made to feel wrong for caring about what happens to you. You matter to me. I care."

In the face of Kyson's adorable outrage, Banks couldn't stop smiling. "Thank you."

Kyson's forehead furrowed. "For what?"

"For being the best part of me."

Kyson visibly melted. "Oh. You're welcome."

A laugh burst from Banks. Kyson honestly deserved better from him. "Do you want to do something today?"

Kyson shrugged. "Like what?"

"I don't know." It was an honest answer. He no longer knew what people did for fun. "Play mini golf. Go see a movie. Find an arcade. You know, a day date."

A smile exploded across Kyson's face. "I would've very much love to have a day date with you."

"Cool." Banks stood and smashed out his cigar in the sink. "Let me get a shower. Think about what you want to do."

"Okay."

The happiness in Kyson's voice had Banks moving his way.

He bent and kissed Kyson's cheek. He could be a better person. Banks would try. He also might kill Shane later. Banks hadn't decided yet. How dare Shane scold Kyson? Banks' shoulders fell. Then again, how could he stay silent? No one besides his family had known him longer than Shane. If anyone knew he wasn't worth loving, it was Shane.

His legs hurt. Banks had burst from his shower wearing a shit-eating grin and with a secret plan. Kyson hadn't been forced to choose an activity. Banks had planned their entire day. Apparently, a hot shower had inspired him. They went to Disneyland.

Kyson had eaten so much, his stomach hurt. His legs ached from all the walking. He was sunburned and tired. Kyson was also happier than he had ever been in his life.

Several times, Banks held his hand. Kyson couldn't stop thinking about that. He also couldn't stop musing over Banks' confession. Everyone left him. Kyson wouldn't. He wouldn't abandon his friend. Except maybe they were also more than friends, and Kyson couldn't stop obsessing over the idea. He loved Banks. Likely, he had for a long time. His feelings were out of his control, so Kyson didn't try to control them. The way that Banks had overtaken his life and cared for him in ways no one ever had, Kyson hadn't stood a chance. There was no fighting it.

"Do you think Soren is cute?"

A nervous-sounding laugh rumbled from Banks. He didn't look away from the road as he drove. "Is this a trick question?"

Kyson smiled. Turned sideways in his seat, he couldn't take his eyes off Banks. He looked so relaxed and sober today. God. Kyson wanted everything from him, especially his thoughts. "No. I'm going somewhere with this. Objectively speaking, do you think he's cute?"

Banks stared straight ahead, looking thoughtful, as if he had never considered it before. "In his own way, yes. He's very angelic-looking and has pretty eyes. Why do you ask? Please tell me you're not trying to set me up."

The jealous rage that sideswiped him nearly stole Kyson's sight. He had to take a breath before he answered. "No. I think he maybe has a crush on Shane. I don't want him to get his feelings hurt. Shane is nice to him, but it's his job to be nice."

"No. It's not. It's his job to keep you safe. That means possibly being very, very not nice." Banks blew out a sigh. "Well, fuck. I suppose I can't kill him now. Your friend will be upset, which will make you upset. Back to square one, I guess."

Confusion crowded Kyson's brain. "What are you talking about? Why would you kill Shane?"

"He made you feel bad. I'm not okay with that." Banks said the words with so much passion, everything inside Kyson lit like a candle.

"You can't kill everyone who makes me feel bad."

Banks glanced over, looking deadly. "I can and will."

Kyson's heart sang. "You're very beautiful." He had no idea where the words came from, but he was absolutely horrified. He refused to take them back, but he had to quickly move on. "Thank you for today. This was amazing."

Banks grabbed his hand and brought it to his mouth, kissing it. "You deserve more of this. I wish I had thought of it sooner."

"And you say you're not a good daddy."

Banks cocked his head to one side. He looked confused.

Kyson's heart sank. "You don't remember saying that." It wasn't a question. It was more than obvious by Banks' expression he had no clue what Kyson talked about.

Banks cast another quick glance his way. "It doesn't matter. If you say I said it, then I did, and it's true. I'm not a good daddy."

"What are you, then?"

Banks smiled and tossed a wink his way. "A deadly one."

"Maybe that's exactly what I need." Fuck. Why did he keep talking? He had already decided he shouldn't get himself into this dynamic again.

Before Kyson had time to panic, Banks pulled to the side of the road. He took full advantage of Kyson's confusion and was across the car before Kyson questioned a thing. His mouth covered Kyson's. It wasn't overwhelming or scary. In fact, it was the sweetest kiss Kyson had ever experienced. He was gentle. The way Banks cupped his face, holding him like he was made of glass, was earth-shattering. His breath hitched.

Banks pulled away and kissed Kyson's forehead.

"You're saving me. You don't see it, but you're saving me."

Something inside Kyson crumbled. He was pretty sure it was the last of the walls he had built after Jack. Kyson didn't think he had saved Banks. Not yet, but he would. Banks would see. Kyson would fix everything.

CHAPTER THREE

AFTER A SHOWER AND a ton of water, Banks felt halfway human. He didn't let himself feel anything very often, but it had been a good day. With the lights out and Kyson tucked against his side, a movie played on the wall. Banks didn't see it. His mind was too busy with other things. That kiss was the biggest thought in his head, followed closely by Shane scolding Kyson. He felt too much tonight. Banks was too sober. He wanted to kiss Kyson again, and he wanted to murder Shane. Then again, Shane wasn't wrong. He was definitely wrong for taking any sort of angry tone with Kyson. He had to know Kyson couldn't handle it. But telling Kyson not to care about Banks was totally fair. Banks wouldn't care about him in Kyson's shoes, but Kyson did, and Banks was determined to deserve it.

The door opened and Shane strolled in, obviously having taken advantage of his day off. He held several shopping bags and looked relaxed. His gaze moved over the way Banks held Kyson. He walked away without as much as a hello. A loud sigh rang through Banks' head. He didn't know how to feel. On one hand, he understood. On the other, fuck. Give him a goddamn chance to fuck up before getting angry. The irritation beat him.

Banks kissed Kyson's temple. "Will it bother you if I light up?"

"Not at all." The open trust in Kyson's voice proved he genuinely didn't care. His heart had never stood a chance. Kyson wanted him as is. That was the hottest fucking thing he had ever experienced. He kept his lips against Kyson's skin, placing several more kisses until Kyson laughed. Banks couldn't stop smiling. The pressure in his chest eased.

"I thought you were lighting up."

Banks' mouth moved to Kyson's ear. He kissed the shell. "I changed my mind. The last thing I want is to prove Shane right."

Kyson leaned away and met Banks' stare. "I don't give a good goddamn what Shane thinks. You're the only one who matters to me. I wouldn't be sitting here right now if I didn't think I could accept you exactly as you are. Do I wish you'd stop trying to kill yourself the way you did last night? Yes, but I've also been here six months and I know that's not normal for you. I trust you not to break my heart like that."

Banks patted his lap. "Come here."

Kyson did as told, straddling Banks' lap.

Banks hauled him closer. "You have nothing to worry about."

Kyson nodded, looking way more trusting than he should. "I know."

"You should definitely kiss me."

Embarrassment tinged Kyson's features, but he still leaned in and touched his lips to Banks'. Banks let him lead. Someone had already taken everything from Kyson once. Banks wanted to give him his power back. While Kyson might have been flustered, he didn't hold back. He nibbled Banks' bottom lip until Banks opened for him. When their tongues met, Banks lost some of his resolve on letting Kyson be in charge. His fingers found the zipper of Kyson's one-piece elephant pajamas. He slid it down, moving slowly in case Kyson wanted him to stop. The moment he slipped his hands beneath the material, he heard Kyson take a shaky breath. Banks' chest swelled. For once, he didn't feel like a failure.

"Your dad is on the phone. He says he's been trying to call for an hour."

Banks dropped his forehead to Kyson's shoulder. "I don't even know where my phone is. Tell him I'm busy."

"I already tried that. He says he has an unwilling guest."

Banks growled. He zipped Kyson's pajamas. "Go pack a bag, baby. We'll stay at Dad's tonight."

Kyson nodded and climbed from his lap without argument. He knew Kyson would rather spend the night in Banks' childhood bedroom than be alone with Shane right now. It was nowhere near the first time they had stayed with his parents. Kyson would be fine there. Banks swore Kyson was the only person his mom liked other than her children. Banks watched Kyson pass Shane with his head down. His eye twitched.

Banks waited until Kyson was out of earshot. "I expect you to apologize to Kyson. Since the moment he stepped foot in this house, he's been nothing but kind. He didn't deserve for you to scold him like that. You know he can't handle it."

"Banks, I—"

Banks swiped a hand through the air. "I don't give a fuck what you think about me. I'm used to everyone in this family thinking I'm a piece of shit. If you can't apologize, or you're unhappy here, you can go back to living with Dad."

Shane's features hardened at the threat. "You know I don't want to live with your dad, and you know I don't think you're a piece of shit. You're fucking killing yourself while the rest of us have to sit back and watch."

"Apologize to Kyson."

"I'd already intended to do so."

Banks dipped his chin. "Then we have nothing else to talk about."

Shane pinched the spot between his eyes. "Your phone is in your car." With that final tidbit, Shane disappeared back down the hall. Banks didn't know how to feel. This was what he got for not lighting up. He shouldn't feel anything at all. Nothing good ever came of his emotions. His temper always won and everyone else paid the price.

Beau Bosi's house was more like an estate. It was huge and imposing. Everything inside was pretentious as hell. The first time Kyson had visited, he had been scared out of his mind. Then he had met Banks' mom, Tabitha. She was eccentric and caustic. Kyson loved her. She loved a family with all her heart that didn't deserve her. Kyson could tell her sons loved her, but Beau was so fucking unbearable, no one wanted to be around him. That left her isolated.

Unfortunately, Kyson hadn't seen Tabitha when they arrived—likely because it was so late. Banks had taken Kyson to his childhood bedroom, found a movie for him to watch, and then headed back downstairs to deal with whatever bullshit Beau dragged him into. Kyson's heart broke for Beau's family. They were his wife and kids, but they were more like hostages.

The more time that passed, the more Kyson's nerves stretched. He chewed the side of his thumbnail and watched the door. Eventually, he dozed. Light and the sound of water running jerked Kyson awake. He spent a moment confused about where he was before spotting Banks standing at the bathroom sink. Blood covered his hands. His discarded shirt on the floor was covered in blood. Kyson couldn't tell if it was his, but he saw the split knuckles even from his vantage point. He slipped from the bed and padded that way. Kyson half expected Banks to close the bathroom door in his face. He didn't. In fact, he stared at nothing with the water running pointlessly. It was as if Banks had disappeared inside himself. Kyson kissed the spot between Banks' shoulder blades. He kept his lips pressed to Banks' skin as he reached around him and led Banks' hands beneath the water. Banks flinched. Kyson made a shushing sound against his skin as he gently washed Banks' hands.

"You shouldn't touch me."

Kyson kept kissing his shoulder, ignoring the words.

"You're too good to be touching someone like me."

The dead note to Banks' voice was breaking his heart. "Turn around." Kyson had gotten his hands as clean as he could without some sort of ointment to stem the bleeding. "Let me see."

To his surprise, Banks obeyed.

Kyson kept his gaze locked on Banks' hands. He had an irrational fear Banks would shut him out if he met his stare. "Is there a first-aid kit around here? Or maybe just some antibacterial ointment?"

"Under the sink."

Kyson worked around him to search the cabinet. He found the kit and went back to working on Banks' hands.

"This is who I'll always be. I don't have a choice."

"I know." Kyson patted the wounds dry with gauze before swiping ointment across his busted knuckles.

"I'm an addict."

He blew on the wounds. "I know."

"You'll never be able to love someone like me."

Kyson lifted his chin. The pain he saw in Banks' eyes nearly buckled his knees. "I already do."

Kyson's feet left the floor as Banks swept him into his arms. "I want to call you a fool, but I'm scared as hell you'll believe me."

His heart never stood a chance against this sexy, broken man. He had saved Kyson, but Kyson thought—maybe—Banks needed him too.

Banks set one knee on the bed and followed Kyson down. He looked so intense, Kyson couldn't look away. "I just want to hold you. There're no condoms or anything here. Not that I'm assuming."

Kyson might have smiled if things didn't feel so powerful between them. "I want to touch you." He had to know what Banks looked like when he came. Kyson thought he might go insane if he didn't do all the things he wanted. He didn't want to wake up tomorrow and realize he lost his chance, or this was just a dream. A temporary bout of insanity on Banks' part.

Banks didn't respond. On his side, facing Kyson, he held Kyson's stare. It was like they couldn't look away from each other.

Kyson skimmed his fingers down Banks' torso, silently begging Banks not to stop him. A flush slowly rose on Banks' cheeks as Kyson unbuttoned and unzipped his pants.

"You're so incredibly beautiful. Inside and out." Banks visibly swallowed as Kyson's fingers encircled his cock. "I'm terrified I'll destroy everything that makes you flawless."

Kyson stroked. "Then don't." It truly felt that simple to Kyson. Kyson didn't want to hurt Banks, so he wouldn't. It should be just as easy for Banks, except Banks had his family looming over him. There would be things he couldn't control.

Banks' lips parted. His breathing turned heavier.

Kyson didn't look away. He wouldn't let Banks' family destroy this. Kyson knew who he loved. He wasn't scared. In fact, he had never felt more protected. Cherished. His body burned, but Kyson didn't care about himself. Of course, that was his problem. He had never cared about himself. Kyson put everyone above himself. He couldn't help it. He just wasn't that special.

Banks slowly slid the zipper down on Kyson's pajamas. Still, his gaze never wavered from holding Kyson's stare. When Banks' hand found its way inside Kyson's underwear, he swallowed. It scared him how good Banks' touch felt. Banks rolled, pinning Kyson beneath him. A small part of Kyson wanted to panic. Nothing good ever happened to him beneath a man. Except Banks never relinquished his stare, and Kyson trusted him. He believed in Banks in a way he never had anyone before. Then

Banks held their cocks together and rolled his hips. A gasp tore from Kyson. No one had ever made love to him. He had zero doubt that was exactly what Banks did.

"Tell me."

Kyson didn't have to question the demand. He knew because he ached for the same. "I love you."

Banks' mouth covered his and his thrusts quickened. He felt so overwhelmed and weak, but in a good way. Kyson didn't have to fear being vulnerable. Banks would take care of him. Kyson forgot to overthink. His body's needs took over his every thought. He was a limp noodle, while everything was done to him, but Kyson couldn't function. All he could do was focus on their kiss and the tension climbing his shaft.

His fingertips dug into Banks' shoulders. He fought the urge to pull him closer. Kyson was ready to fly apart at the seams. Banks leaned his head away and visibly strained toward release. The taut lines on his face sent Kyson over the edge. He had done that. Kyson was the reason for that ecstasy. The knowledge had him shaking and whimpering as cum filled the space between them.

Then Banks dropped his chin. His expression was crystal clear and lucid. "I love you." The confession rocked Kyson's soul as Banks shook cum out onto his skin. Kyson's mind stayed frozen on those three little words. They bounced around his brain like a bullet on the loose. Nothing mattered but knowing he owned Banks' heart. Kyson didn't give a shit about anything else anymore. He was exactly where he was meant to be. Let it destroy him. He no longer cared.

CHAPTER FOUR

UNFORTUNATELY, THEY HADN'T BEEN allowed to sneak away before the house roused for the day. They had been forced to join the family in the garden for brunch, which was really just crepes and mimosas. So many mimosas. From there, Banks had to take care of a few things, leaving Kyson alone with Tabitha. That would have been perfect, except Beau was there... with his live-in whore, Adan.

Adan was beautiful, and he knew it. Kyson hated his stupid face. What kind of man moved in with a married man and flaunted their affair in his wife's face? A little bitch, that's who. Kyson always fought the urge to punch him. Instead, he donned himself in shy armor, hoping it kept Adan at arm's length.

Kyson sat at the table with Tabitha. His chair sat barely an inch from hers. With their shoulders touching, Kyson held her hand beneath the table. Beau drew hopscotch on the nearby tennis court for Adan. Adan smiled and laughed as he hopped through each square.

Tabitha lifted her glass to her lips. "I hate him."

"Which one?" Kyson was genuinely curious who she blamed for this hell she endured.

"Both of them."

Since she started the conversation, Kyson dove in with both feet. "Why don't you leave? You're so incredibly beautiful. Anyone would be lucky to have you and would treat you like a queen."

A sad smile passed over her lips. "There's only one way to leave this family." Her gaze slid Kyson's way. "You know that goes for you as well, right?"

Kyson nodded. His eyes were wide open. He no longer cared about the cost. He had paid a higher price for less.

Tabitha patted his hand. "Good. Banks is pretty well split between his father and me. Unfortunately, I think he got the worst of both of us. All my addictions with his father's terrifying temper."

"He got love from somewhere too." Kyson didn't have to think about it. The words simply fell from his lips. "He has so much amazingly beautiful love inside him. I think he has more of you than you realize."

Tabitha's eyes filled with tears. She turned her head, blinking rapidly while watching her husband give everything to someone else. Kyson had never felt so much rage on someone else's behalf. He wished with everything he had he could save her. As always, Kyson was completely helpless. He couldn't make anything better.

Banks appeared at his side, with Kyson's backpack slung over his shoulder. "Are you ready?"

Kyson looked Tabitha's way. He would stay if she needed him.

She patted his hand again. "It was good to see you, sweetie. Go enjoy your day."

He hugged her.

She chuckled, but hugged him back.

Banks kissed her cheek. "Thank you for brunch." His gaze moved toward where his dad and Adan played. A muscle flexed in his jaw. Kyson knew he bit back all the words. He met Tabitha's stare again. "Would you like to come home with me? You can hang out with Kyson, and Shane hasn't seen you in a while."

A sad smile passed over her lips. "Thank you, but you know I can't."

The muscle in Banks' jaw worked double time.

She squeezed his hand. "Go. Be young."

Kyson's throat swelled. She was young too. Tabitha deserved better than this. Kyson had no clue how Banks withstood the rage. The fury inside Kyson was massive, and he had only known Tabitha for six months. How had Banks stood this for years? He forced himself to stand and kiss her cheek. Kyson couldn't make her leave any more than he could have escaped Jack without Banks. As Tabitha had said, sometimes, there was only one way out.

"Call me if you need me."

She smiled. "Of course."

Banks took his hand and led him to the car. Kyson tried not to cry the whole way home. It was obvious how well Banks knew him. He didn't talk, leaving Kyson to hang on to his dignity. If he opened his mouth, the anger and tears of frustration would flow. He understood Banks better each time they saw his parents. Kyson kind of wanted to get high and stay that way. The alternative was to kill Beau and Adan. Since that was impossible, then what? Nothing. Helplessness. He wanted to smash some shit.

Kyson walked through the club, seeing nothing. Banks let him inside their home. Kyson headed for his bedroom with his backpack squeezed against his chest. He needed to unpack. As he dumped everything on the bed, Shane appeared in the doorway. Kyson bit back the urge to scream. He couldn't deal with Shane right now.

"I need to apologize to you."

Kyson hadn't expected that. He didn't know what to say.

Shane kept going. "I shouldn't have taken my frustration out on you the other night. You didn't deserve it."

The fight bled from Kyson. Frustration was something Kyson understood all too well. He imagined Shane felt the same way watching Banks kill himself as Kyson did watching Tabitha. "I understand. You don't want me enabling him."

Shane swiped a hand over his eyes. "I don't know that it's even that. It's just—"

"You feel helpless," Kyson finished for him. "You're watching him kill himself and there's nothing you can do. Part of you wonders if he's even wrong for it."

Shane gave him a sharp nod.

Kyson sat on the edge of his bed and held Shane's stare. "You're not wrong to feel all those things. While I feel the same way, I'm also determined to love him no matter what every step of the way, because you know what? No one else has, and that's a huge part of the problem." Kyson shoved his clasped hands between his knees so Shane wouldn't see the way they shook. While this wasn't exactly a confrontation, Kyson had stopped being able to have conversations like this a long time ago. He had been beaten into submission and fear. This was too important, though. "He's used to being everyone's disappointment. There's no reason for him to fight. Everyone is just waiting for the day he turns up dead, so why should he bother? He should care because I'm here waiting. I love him and I need him to come home. If he doesn't wake up tomorrow, it'll kill me. Banks needs someone to feel that way. Since life has already stripped everything from me, I'm the perfect person for the job. I have nothing to lose except him. So I don't really give a fuck if you judge me for it."

A smile exploded across Shane's face. "You're pretty tough for a Little."

Pain sliced through Kyson. He shook his head. "I wear the clothes, play with the toys, and go through the motions. But I don't find comfort in being a Little anymore and I don't know if I ever will again. Everything inside me is just defeated."

With his shoulder leaned against the doorframe and his arms crossed over his chest, Shane stared at Kyson like he saw him. It was exposing, yet oddly freeing. Shane straightened. "Well, it seems you're more perfect for Banks than even you know. I'm glad he has you."

A weak smile pulled at Kyson's lips. It had been nerve-wracking, but he was glad they had this conversation. He hated walking on eggshells. Maybe he hadn't solved anything inside himself, but he still felt better. Now he wanted Banks to hold him. He was a mental mess.

Banks leaned against the wall inside his bedroom, just out of sight. He listened to every word. His chest hurt. He honestly didn't know how to feel. Nothing was said Banks didn't know in his heart, but still. It demolished him to hear aloud how much damage Jack had done. He felt such a mixture of pride in Kyson's strength and heartbreak for knowing how deeply Banks always hurt everyone who loved him. But he heard how much Kyson loved him and couldn't doubt him. There was too much power behind the way his voice shook. Banks couldn't lose him the way he had everyone else. He equally couldn't handle his emotions today. Banks fought the urge to trash the house and find every loose pill. He wanted to tear off his skin.

His hands shook as he tapped a laced cigar from its packaging. It was the tamest drug he used. Banks just needed to take the edge off and forget the way Kyson had stared at his mother with so much pain. He knew that look. It matched how he always felt: fucking helpless. He was completely fucking useless in the face of every single sin of his father's making. Banks was just like his mom. When he saw the way she never left the house, or stayed sober even for a second, he saw his future and he hated it. Banks just didn't know how to avoid that outcome.

He lit up and inhaled.

Kyson appeared in the doorway.

Banks almost snuffed out the cigar immediately in guilt, except Kyson smiled like his whole day brightened because he set eyes on Banks. He snuffed out the cigar because he wanted both hands free for his baby.

"Come here." He lifted Kyson from his feet and headed for bed. "I think you need to be cuddled."

Kyson held his stare, looking sweet and innocent. "I really do."

God, he was so in love with this man. He was everything Banks needed. Maybe he stood no chance of not being an addict, but he still felt more human with Kyson around. Kyson was the only thing he wanted more than the drugs. That was saying more than even Kyson knew. He had given up a long time ago. Now there was a spark inside him Kyson fanned every day. The moment he had Kyson settled in his arms, Banks could breathe. There was no pressure sitting on his chest. The weight of the world disappeared.

He kissed Kyson's temple. "You are my whole world. You know that, right?"

He swore he heard Kyson smile. "Same."

Banks held him tighter. People claimed love wasn't enough to save anyone. Banks disagreed. Kyson was the only thing saving him. Without him, there was nothing but an early grave. Whatever it took, he would be the perfect daddy. Kyson deserved the best.

CHAPTER FIVE

AT THE PLAYPEN, KYSON had a certain group
of friends he always played with. They didn't
seem to be around as often since Jupiter
married Boone and Luca married Jarek.
Soren was always around to hang out with
Kyson, but it was rare for the four of them
to be together. Kyson was thrilled to have
their little group back together for a game of
Jenga.

In the corner, on the floor, they sat in a
circle, taking turns and laughing every time
they had to start over. Kyson desperately

wanted to tell them about Banks. It had been several weeks since he had moved his things to Banks' bedroom. He was happier than he had ever been and really wanted to share it with someone. Each time he opened his mouth to get started, his face flushed. They weren't a secret. He just kind of liked keeping Banks to himself. Kyson wasn't ready to share.

"I'm so happy everyone is here. We never get to see each other anymore. As a group, I mean."

Soren nodded at Kyson's words. He focused on Jupiter and Luca. "Married life must keep you two busy. You're never here anymore."

Luca laughed. "To be fair, Daddy works long hours, so I usually play at his office."

"All alone?" Jupiter sounded horrified.

Luca blushed. "Well, sometimes, it's fun to be alone... with Daddy."

They roared with laughter, making Luca blush redder and heads turn their way. Kyson met Banks' stare. They didn't look away. Heat built between them.

Soren bumped shoulders with him, reminding Kyson it was his turn.

He bit his bottom lip and carefully pulled a block from the tower. Kyson blew out a sigh when the blocks didn't collapse. The club went quiet for half a second. Just long enough to pull all eyes toward the door. Beau strolled into the club with a pouty-looking Adan. Littles immediately turned their backs, making it clear they wanted no part of him. Since Jupiter married Boone, all the Littles knew the story of Adan. Everyone liked Jupiter. That meant they hated Adan for loyalty's sake.

Beau steered Adan toward their group and then left him to sit with Boone, Banks, and Jarek. For a moment, Adan stared at them sullenly. His bright green eyes flashed with resentment. Luca stood and grabbed his backpack, leaving the group without saying goodbye. He headed straight for his daddy. After a moment, Jarek stood, and the pair made their way toward the door. Luca waved over his shoulder. Kyson bit the inside of his cheek to keep from laughing. Luca and Boone were friends. He had Luca's loyalty forever. In no world would Luca play with Adan.

Adan tried to turn away and sit with Beau. Beau swatted him on the butt, sending him away. This time, Adan came back twice as sullen. He plopped down where Luca had been. With his arms crossed over his chest, he stared at the floor.

They exchanged glances.

Soren being Soren, and too nice for his own good, he tried including Adan. "We have a spot open, if you'd like to take Luca's place."

Adan narrowed his eyes at Soren. "I don't need a fat Little, who no one wants, to pity play with me." He kicked over their Jenga tower.

Fury slammed into Kyson at the hurt on Soren's face. Soren gathered his things, as if he meant to leave. The rage just kept getting deeper and deeper. All Adan did was hurt people. Kyson fucking hated him.

Something snapped inside Kyson. He was tired of being weak. "Home-wrecking little bitch." Kyson's fist shot out and connected with Adan's eye. It stunned Adan just enough for Kyson to launch himself on Adan. He didn't stop scratching and hitting him until he was physically lifted away. Rage coated his vision, but he didn't miss the way Beau sat back, smoking and smiling like the evil bastard he was.

"Take him home." Banks sounded enraged.

That deflated Kyson and made him realize Shane was the one who held him off the ground. He spotted Soren heading for the door. Kyson twisted. "I'll go home. Just go after Soren. Adan said something really horrible to him. He needs someone more than me. I'll behave." Even Kyson heard the desperation in his voice. He couldn't let Soren leave upset.

Shane looked visibly torn. Finally, he headed for home with Kyson tucked beneath one arm.

"Seriously, Shane. You can trust me to find my way without you."

"Hush." The grumbled word held so much fury, Kyson immediately fell silent. "You just attacked Beau's boy. If I don't make a show of this until we're out of sight, it might be him who comes after you."

Fuck. Kyson hadn't thought of that. He dutifully let Shane haul him out of sight. The moment they weren't visible to the table, Shane set Kyson on his feet. Kyson shooed him away and headed for the safety of home. Reality got a little realer by the second. What the fuck had he just done? What would Beau do? His stomach hurt. With the adrenaline wearing off, he realized a few things hurt. His knuckles ached. There were scratches on his arm. He might have just lost Banks. At just the thought, Kyson's knees gave out. He sat hard on the coffee table. Kyson couldn't lose Banks. He had nothing else.

Soren stood in the foyer of The PlayPen and stripped. He couldn't leave wearing his pajamas. Not only was it nearing record high temperatures for March outside, but he also thought—maybe—he was done. Maybe it was time for the shorts and t-shirt beneath his pajamas to be his full-time persona. Adan was right. No one wanted a fat Little. Every time he came here, he fed into a need that would never be met. All the men here wanted a tiny twink that fit their fantasy's description. He would never be that. The sad part was, Soren was only unhappy with himself when he was here. Today just proved he needed to give up this dream.

"Where are you going?"

At Shane's appearance, Soren nearly fell over, trying to get his foot out of his pajamas.

Shane rushed forward to steady him.

Soren couldn't look at him. "Thanks. I think it's best if I leave."

"Why? What did that asshole say to you?"

Soren stayed focused on folding his pajamas and trying to stuff them in his backpack. "Nothing I didn't already know."

Shane took away the backpack and the pajamas, forcing Soren to look at him. "Tell me."

The pleading in his cute hazel eyes only made Soren feel worse. The humiliation was too much. Tears of frustration welled in his eyes, horrifying him beyond reason.

"Tell me," Shane repeated, sounding like he genuinely cared.

"He said he doesn't need a fat Little like me, who no one wants, to pity play with him." Soren's voice shook with the confession. He fucking hated that. Soren didn't want to be this person. He wanted to be brave.

Rage flared in Shane's eyes. That was all the warning Soren got before Shane snagged the front of his t-shirt and hauled him forward. His mouth covered Soren's. Soren melted. There was no other way to describe what happened to his body. It went limp. Shane's arms were the only thing keeping him upright. He was everything Soren had fantasized he would be: strong and bold. Soren didn't even care that it was a pity kiss. His knees shook from the powerful emotions filling his chest. He had wanted this for so long. So much longer than anyone could guess.

Shane pulled away. He swiped the moisture from Soren's bottom lip while holding his stare. "You should probably knee me in the balls now for manhandling you."

"I still know Judo." Soren had no idea why he said such a stupid thing, but his brain refused to work.

A huge smile exploded across Shane's face. He pressed the pajamas into Soren's arms. "Put these back on. Don't you dare let him win. Plus, I imagine Kyson will need you soon. When he fully realizes the ass he just kicked belongs to Beau, he'll likely crack."

Nothing could have gotten Soren back in his pajamas faster. Kyson had stood up for him in a way no one ever had. He was Soren's best friend. Soren wouldn't let him face the music alone.

Boone and Banks kept exchanging glances. Banks knew Boone had his back if their dad exploded. Still, Banks was too sober for this. He had cut back to only smoking his laced cigars. There weren't nearly enough drugs in those to deal with taking on his father today. No way in hell would he let his dad harm his baby. There were lines even his father wasn't allowed to cross.

Beau puffed on his cigar and eyed Banks.

Banks kept his face blank. He knew better than to show an ounce of weakness. Plus, Banks recognized his power too. He was the one his dad turned to when he needed someone to disappear. Banks imagined they were on equal footing.

"Well, you've definitely got a scrapper there, boy. Looks like he'll fit right in with our bunch."

Adan huffed from his chair next to Beau. He still held an ice pack against his eye. "Daddy, he hit me."

Beau shot him an annoyed look. "I saw. I also saw you start it. Never pick a fight you can't finish."

Adan went back to pouting.

Boone stood. "My husband and I have dinner reservations." He nodded at everyone and left Banks with the drama. Banks couldn't blame him. Adan had been engaged to Boone before Boone caught him cheating with their dad. He couldn't imagine how Boone felt every time he saw the two together. It had nothing to do with Adan. He loved his husband more than life. But Boone shouldn't have to endure a betrayal like that from family.

Banks decided to pretend as if nothing happened. "What brought you by tonight?"

"Your mother said she wanted the house to herself for a few hours. We had some time to kill before dinner. I thought I'd see my boys."

Banks nodded. At least his dad had respected his mom's wishes on something. They owned a huge estate, but it seemed as if his dad always purposely tracked her down with Adan in tow. He never gave her a moment's peace from his open affair. The saddest part was, if his mom ever so much as looked at another man, that guy would be dead on the spot. Yet his father spent every day tormenting her. Banks needed a drink.

He motioned for a server.

The guy didn't hesitate to bring Banks a Jack and Coke. He put the glass to his lips and immediately set it back down without drinking. The smell turned his stomach, and Kyson needed him clearheaded.

Beau checked his watch. "We should probably head out for dinner as well, so I can grab something for your mom too while we're out. Otherwise, she'll choose not to eat if we stay out too late."

Banks' gaze slid Adan's way. It was out of his control. More times than he could count, Banks had wondered how Adan truly felt about this arrangement. The guy was pushing thirty. He had lived as Beau's whore for ten years. Surely, he harbored some sort of resentment or anything at all. The dude obviously had no shame or pride. Not to mention his lack of care for others, but goddamn. Did he feel nothing? Adan's gaze was locked on his lap, stealing Banks' chance to get a read on him.

"It was good seeing you, Dad."

Beau stood and squeezed his shoulder before heading toward the door with Adan in tow.

Banks counted to ten and then went in search of Kyson. He didn't want to look too eager. His dad might reappear any second, and Beau Bosi excelled at destroying things. Before he made it to the hallway that led to his personal space, the door to the club opened and Axton stepped inside. Banks froze. He had given Axton free passes to check out the place, but the guy had never taken him up on the offer.

His eerie light gaze slid across the room before landing on Banks. A smile touched his lips. He closed the distance between them. "Hey."

Banks couldn't help but smile. He genuinely liked Axton. "Hey. I honestly never expected to see you here."

Axton looked around again. "Yeah. It's not really my scene, but I get bored sometimes." He focused on Banks again. "I hadn't heard from you in a while. As fucked up as you were the last time I saw you, I worried you were dead somewhere."

Banks chuckled. "Nah. I've just been busy." He motioned for Axton to follow. "Come on." Banks made his way down the hallway until he reached his door. He half expected to find Kyson in tears. Axton's visit was inconvenient timing, but he could hardly boot the guy from the building when he'd come to check on Banks. He opened the door to chaos. The living room furniture had been pushed against the walls and the tent was back. Pillows surrounded a tiny indoor s'mores maker. Shane, Kyson, and Soren were all in their pajamas, taking turns toasting marshmallows.

A smile exploded across Banks' face. "What's going on here? Are you having a camp-out without me?"

Kyson beamed at him. He patted a pillow beside him. "I saved you a seat. Go put your pjs on."

Banks stepped farther into the room, revealing Axton behind him. "This is my friend, Axton. Axton, you know Shane, of course."

Shane gave him a nod, greeting him.

Banks motioned toward Soren. "This is Soren, and," he moved to Kyson's side and sat, "this is my baby, Kyson."

"Take your shoes off. You'll get the pillows dirty."

"Oops." Banks pulled off his shoes and tossed them aside at Kyson's reminder. He stole a kiss before focusing on Axton again.

Axton looked uncomfortable and unsure of his welcome.

Kyson motioned toward an empty pillow. "Come on. We have plenty."

Even though he still looked like he might bail, Axton tugged off his biker boots and awkwardly sat on the pillow on the floor. He looked out of place as hell in his leather pants and tattoos. No one batted an eye. He openly eyed Kyson. "What happened to your hand?"

Until Axton posed the question, Banks hadn't noticed Kyson's knuckles were bandaged.

Kyson blushed. "I beat up Banks' dad's affair partner."

Axton's eyebrows lifted. "And you lived to tell about it?"

Kyson shifted nervously, but didn't respond.

Banks answered for him. "First off, no one, not even my dad, is about to lay one god-damn finger on my baby."

Kyson stroked his thigh.

Banks continued. "But you also know my dad. He's a cold-hearted bastard. I'm pretty sure he thought the whole thing was funny. He told Adan not to pick a fight he couldn't finish next time."

Shane laughed.

Axton eyed Kyson again before focusing on Banks. "I take it Adan is the affair partner."

"Home-wrecking little bitch," Kyson muttered under his breath.

Banks bit his bottom lip to keep from laughing. Once he had himself under control, he answered. "Yeah." He turned his head and focused on Kyson. "What happened, by the way?"

Kyson had just taken a bite of his s'more, so he couldn't answer.

Banks grabbed a napkin and wiped the melted chocolate from his face while he chewed.

He swallowed. "He said something he shouldn't have."

Axton laughed. "Well, I guess he'll think before he speaks next time."

"Probably not," Banks, Kyson, and Shane said simultaneously.

Everyone laughed.

Axton's shoulders relaxed.

Kyson cocked his head to one side and studied Axton. "Why do you look slightly familiar to me?"

Axton shrugged.

Banks filled him in. "He's Jarek's younger brother."

"Oh, yeah," Kyson cried. "I see it now. You two have different colorations, but your face is very similar."

Banks had never really noticed that before, but Kyson was right.

Axton only nodded. He wasn't on the best of terms with his older lawyer brother. Banks had never really understood why. He assumed they were just too different.

"We should get drunk and play Truth or Dare."

Everyone looked at Soren at his suggestion.

Soren shrugged. "I think we've earned it."

A laugh burst from Kyson.

Shane pushed to his feet. "I'll grab the game board."

Kyson jumped to his feet. "Can I run to the bar and grab the liquor, Daddy?"

Banks' throat swelled so fast and unexpectedly, it took him a second to recover. It was the first time Kyson had called him Daddy without stopping himself. Kyson sounded so much like the Little he had been before Jack that Banks nearly teared up. It was like he had healed someone. Him. That meant Kyson truly was saving him. "Of course, baby. Get whatever you want for the group. The guys know to give you anything you want."

Kyson did a cute, happy clap.

Soren stood too. "Can I come? I know it was my idea, but you know I don't really like the taste of alcohol. Maybe I can find something tolerable."

Kyson linked his arm through Soren's and steered toward the door. "Good idea. Maybe they'll have a suggestion for you."

They disappeared, chatting, and leaving Banks alone with Axton.

Axton cleared his throat. "So, you're a daddy. I knew you owned this place, but I still never pictured that about you. Is this why I haven't seen you in a while?"

Banks didn't know what to make of Axton's words or tone. He sounded oddly serious. Banks decided to be fully honest, especially since he always got his most fucked up when they were together. "The last time we went out, I don't know how I made it home. I scared Kyson. He had to be the one who kept me from choking on my own vomit on the bathroom floor. I don't know, man. The idea of failing him like that. It doesn't sit right with me. In his heart, he's a Little. He should never be the caretaker. There's something fucked up in me." Banks knew he wasn't explaining himself well. They never had meaningful discussions. Banks didn't like being serious.

"He deserves better. I get it."

Banks' shoulders relaxed. "Exactly. If anything were to happen to me, all this would become his. But he's not equipped for that, and I don't want to force him to be that person." The way it was forced on Banks. "I love him. He needs me to be better."

Axton nodded.

Shane returned with the game board. Banks had a feeling he had been hovering out of sight, letting Banks have his private conversation and waiting for his chance to return without it being awkward. Shane focused on Axton as he reclaimed his pillow on the floor. "Are you up for this?"

Axton shrugged. "Why not? I've got nowhere else to be."

It hit Banks. Axton likely didn't feel like he had anyone. The guy barely spoke to his brother. The biker gang he had done time for were still around, but ten years in prison was a long time. Things changed. Feelings changed.

Kyson and Soren returned laughing and arms laden with bottles.

Soren shook a glass canister. "They mixed me a whole bottle of something called a Buttery Nipple."

Shane groaned.

Soren's face fell. "What? Is it nasty?"

Shane shook his head. "It's good, but it's sweet. Don't make yourself sick."

The smile returned to Soren's face. "Oh. I'll try. But throwing up is still probably less embarrassing than me showing off my sick dance moves."

Shane chuckled and shook his head.

Banks looked between the two. Kyson was right. Soren did have a crush, and judging by Shane's smile, it wasn't one-sided.

After reclaiming their spots, they set their haul on the floor. Kyson tried arranging the bottles where they were easy to reach for everyone. "I didn't know what everyone liked." He pushed a bottle of Coke and Jack Banks' way. "Except you, of course."

Banks didn't touch it. "Thanks, baby."

Kyson beamed.

Axton sat forward and eyed the haul. He reached for Banks' bottles. "Do you mind? We have similar tastes."

Banks flashed him a grateful smile. "Go for it. I'll catch up later."

Axton winked and filled one of the Solo cups Soren supplied.

Shane grabbed a bottle of vodka. "I'll just drink from the bottle. I'm the only vodka person."

Kyson nodded. He held up his bottle of wine. "Then, same."

With everyone having their chosen drinks, they rearranged things to have the game board in the center.

Soren explained as Shane ensured the board was set up properly with each person having a Truth or Dare pie slice facing their direction. "Okay. All you have to do is flick the little arrow thing and if it lands on your truth or dare, then that's what you have to do. Simple."

Axton's eyebrows rose. "Who gets to choose what truth or dare we have to do?"

"We just take turns," Kyson explained. "That way, there's no pressure on anyone who can't think of anything to do." Kyson looked around. "Who wants to go first?"

Banks wrapped his arm around Kyson's waist. "I think you should."

Kyson shrugged and flicked the arrow. It landed on Soren.

Soren was mid drink. His shoulders fell when it landed on truth. "Oh, dear."

An evil-sounding laugh fell from Banks' lips before he could stop it. He saw his chance. "Do you have a crush on anyone?"

Soren blushed hard. "Yes."

It was impossible not to miss the way Shane went still.

Soren immediately flicked the arrow before anyone asked him who. It landed on Banks for truth. Soren sat forward so fast to focus on Banks, Banks wondered if he pulled a muscle in his back. "What are your intentions with my best friend?"

Kyson looked horrified.

Everyone else looked curious.

Banks didn't even hesitate. "I hope one of these days, he'll give in and marry me."

Everyone looked shocked except Axton.

Axton merely nodded and flicked the arrow. It landed on Soren again, but for dare.

"Oh, dear."

Banks laughed at his reaction. "This was your idea."

He didn't have time to respond before Shane shouted, "Show us your sick dance moves," and then proceeded to fire up some music on his phone.

Soren covered his face with both hands, but then dutifully stood.

Every face was turned his way and smiling.

Even blushing brightly, Soren fulfilled his dare. To Banks' shock, he was truly badass. He had the moves he claimed. After a few seconds, he reclaimed his pillow. His face couldn't get redder.

Shane shook his head. "Holy shit. That was amazing."

An uncomfortable-sounding chuckle fell from Soren's lips. "It was Dad who made me take Judo. My mom put me in dance."

"Well, I'm impressed," Banks said before flicking the arrow. It landed on truth for Shane. Banks didn't miss a beat. "Do you have a crush on anyone?"

"Yes." He looked serious as hell.

Kyson squeezed his thigh. A silent message passed between them. They would have to do something to get these two together.

Soren and Shane both deserved all the happiness in the world, and they would look good together. Banks would find a way to make it happen.

CHAPTER SIX

WITH AXTON CRASHED OUT in one of the guest rooms, and Soren and Shane playing cards, Kyson finally had Banks alone. Kyson sat on the bed, watching Banks just inside the bathroom removing the makeup he had been dared to wear. He was sexy as hell in eyeliner. It hadn't gone without notice that Banks hadn't touched a drop of alcohol. Kyson was proud of him, but he thought it best to play dumb. He didn't expect Banks to go stone cold sober. That wasn't Banks, and

Kyson had fallen in love with him exactly as he was.

"Are you mad I hit Adan?"

Banks glanced his way. "Are you joking? He's had that coming for a long time."

Kyson shrugged. "Maybe, but I'd never do anything to hurt you. Your dad could've reacted badly, and I didn't think."

Banks patted his face dry and moved Kyson's way. He kept coming until he crawled onto the mattress, tumbled Kyson onto his back, and straddled Kyson. His dark expression had Kyson breathing harder. Everything about him turned Kyson on. With his hands braced on either side of Kyson's head, he held Kyson's stare. "My dad is dangerous, but so am I. You should know by now I would never let anyone hurt you."

Kyson ran his hands up Banks' torso. "I wasn't worried about my safety. There's nothing he could do to me that would be worse than losing you."

"I will never let that happen." Banks lowered his head and skimmed his lips across Kyson's mouth, teasing him with the softest kiss. "You're amazing." He stole another light kiss. "And adorable." Banks nibbled his chin. "And edible."

Kyson laughed at his antics. "You're silly."

Banks sat back on his heels, feigning outrage. "Me? Silly? I'll show you silly." Banks found Kyson's most ticklish spot and tortured him.

Kyson twisted and fought to get away while laughing and begging for mercy. The moment he was face down and pinned beneath Banks, Banks went still. His mouth found Kyson's neck. He sucked. A moan slipped from Kyson. Banks' hands slipped beneath Kyson. He tugged the zipper of his pajamas down before peeling it over his shoulders. His mouth followed every inch of newly bared skin. He continued his descent, dragging Kyson's pajamas off while trapping Kyson's arms in the material. Kyson kept his eyes closed and savored every sensation. He felt worshipped.

Banks reached his ass. "Mmm. Police car underwear. Nice choice." He grabbed the waistband of Banks' underwear and peeled them off along with his onesie.

Cool air brushed his skin, making goosebumps rise. Banks didn't leave him cold for long. Only long enough to strip and suit up. Kyson listened to it all without moving or looking. He let everything happen to him. It was nice handing over control without fear. Kyson knew Banks would never hurt him.

Banks' body covered him again. He went back to kissing Kyson's neck and nape while his wet fingers found Kyson's asshole. "I'm so proud of you."

A stuttered breath escaped Kyson at the praise.

Banks didn't stop. "You're so strong and brave." His fingers were replaced with something much bigger. "I'm honored as hell to be your daddy." He thrust.

Kyson lost his breath. He grasped the blanket beneath him and held on. Love and lust rushed through his veins. Banks' arms wrapped around him, holding him in a cocoon while making shallow thrusts. Kyson focused on every nuance. He whimpered. His body ached. Banks didn't give him more than the sweetest rocking motion. It felt good, but Kyson wanted more.

"Please, Daddy."

"Please, Daddy, what? Ask for what you want."

"Fuck me."

At his demand, Kyson was dragged to his knees. Banks pounded him. Kyson had to hold on. Sounds came from the back of his throat he couldn't control.

"That's it, baby boy. Show Daddy how to come."

Kyson hadn't felt like the Little he was in a long time before today. Banks was slowly giving him himself back. He grew and got stronger every day because Banks loved and accepted him. Kyson would always do the same. He would walk through hell for Banks. Kyson would definitely come when told. He focused everything on the building pressure climbing his cock.

"Come on, baby. Make Daddy's cock spit."

Kyson blew. He buried his face and cried out against the mattress, muffling the sound.

"Fuck, Kyson. You're killing me. This tight little asshole is going to break me. God-damn." A pained sound cut through the air, followed by a loud moan.

Kyson sucked air against the mattress, trying to catch his breath after the powerful or-gasm. Banks fell forward, squashing Kyson against the mattress and pressing him into the mess he had made. Kyson didn't care. He savored the way Banks fought for air against his skin. There was so much love in his heart, it had nowhere to go. He had thought this kind of love was only true in his fantasies. Now he didn't know how he had lived this long without it.

Banks couldn't stop kissing Kyson's nape. He was addicted. Even the smell of Kyson's skin got him high. He had forgotten what it felt like to feel alive before Kyson landed in his life. Now he didn't know how he ever lived without him. Truthfully, he hadn't. All his emotions had been muted for years. Now all he felt was this overwhelming love.

"I love you so much." Banks couldn't hold back the confession.

"I love you too."

Banks smiled as Kyson gave back the words. He knew they were true. Banks wasn't sure he could say that about anyone other than his brother and that wasn't really something they said to each other. They should. Banks should do that.

"Are you okay? I swear I can hear you over-thinking,"

Banks' smile grew bigger at the claim. "Yeah, I'm good. I was just thinking about the day you came to live with me. Before everything happened with—God, I hate saying his name—Jack, you were at that tea party. You wore that cute bat onesie you have. When you told me you were a fruit bat and ate that grape—like an adorable munchkin—that's the moment I knew you were mine. It's crazy. I can't really explain it. Everything happened so fast. One second, I was thinking how fucking adorable you are. The next, I saw your bruises." Banks paused to swallow his rage at only the memory.

"I genuinely might've killed that guy if you hadn't been watching. The only reason I could stop hitting him was I didn't want you to look at me like a monster. I mean, I know I am one."

Kyson rolled so fast, he nearly knocked Banks' teeth out. "You're not. You're the most amazing person I've ever met."

That was sad. "I am a monster." Banks said the words plainly. Kyson needed to understand they were true. "That's kind of my point. I don't know how, but I knew you were mine that day. Thank you for seeing me and loving me anyhow."

"Don't thank me for something that's literally the easiest fucking thing I've ever done in my life." There was no arguing with the power in Kyson's voice. He meant it and Banks knew it. That was why he was so obsessed.

The door burst open. "Why aren't you answering your goddamn phone?"

"Whoa. Whoa. Whoa." Banks grabbed a handful of blankets and quickly covered Kyson. Even though it was just Boone, no one was allowed to look at his man, especially in such a vulnerable position. "Why in the hell are you crashing into my bedroom in the middle of the night?"

Boone's dark hair was a mess. There were dark circles under his eyes. He looked scared and enraged. Broken. "I've been trying to call."

Banks didn't bother looking around for his phone. He didn't know where it was half the time. "What's happened?" Banks knew in his heart it was bad. Boone would never show up like this otherwise.

"It's Mom."

Banks' heart dropped into his stomach. Boone didn't have to say the words. "How?" He needed to know if it was time to kill their dad.

"She sent Dad out tonight."

Banks knew that. They'd had the conversation earlier.

Boone visibly swallowed. "Then she took her own life."

Everything inside Banks ceased to function. There were no thoughts, or maybe there were too many, and he couldn't catch them. Either way, he simply shut down. He barely felt Kyson's arms encircle him.

"I'll get dressed." The words sounded like they came from a stranger.

Boone nodded and closed the door, leaving him to his shock.

Banks still didn't move. Finally, he felt Kyson's tears on his skin. Banks focused on him. Kyson was the only safe place for his brain. He gathered Kyson into his arms and cuddled him. It was almost second nature to comfort Kyson. He wanted to claim he couldn't believe it, but his mom had been working on killing herself one way or another for years.

"We should get dressed. Your family needs you."

Banks stared at Kyson's tear-streaked face and his open pain. "You're my family." The words just automatically fell from his lips. His body was on autopilot, with no one at the helm.

Kyson stroked his chest. He sniffed. "I am, but your brother needs you more right now." He sat up and rolled from the bed. Kyson took Banks' hands and urged him to his feet. He steered Banks to the bathroom and went to work cleaning them up before finding Banks some clothes.

Banks stood like a statue and let Kyson handle him like a doll. He had no idea how long it took, but they were both in jeans and a t-shirt by the time Kyson finished. Then they stood staring at each other. Kyson looked as lost as he felt. Yet, he still cared for Banks like a toddler.

"What do I do now?" Banks didn't know if he meant he didn't know how to use his legs or if he meant he didn't know how to handle this. Both, he supposed. The only thing Banks knew was Kyson would take care of him. They were a family. It's what they did.

CHAPTER SEVEN

SHANE TOOK SOREN HOME in Banks' car. Axton took Shane's keys to the SUV and drove everyone to Beau's place. It was completely silent in the car. Banks imagined Axton was uncomfortable as fuck, but he didn't show it. He had to focus on anything at all except reality. Axton pulled into the circular drive. As his headlights swept the porch, Banks spotted Adan. On the front steps, in a pair of bunny pajamas, he sat with his head down and a suitcase at his feet.

They silently piled out of the SUV. Adan's head didn't lift until they neared. His eyes and nose were red. He looked a mess.

"Daddy put me out." He twisted his fingers. "I don't have anywhere to go. I don't have anything. Nothing. I don't even know how to call an Uber and I don't have any money even if I did." He sounded so distraught, even Banks didn't have the heart to kick him. The guy had been a kept pet his entire adult life. He didn't know how to be anything else.

Boone and Jupiter walked past him like he wasn't even there. They didn't even stick around for the entire speech.

Kyson looked at Banks.

Axton cleared his throat. "I've got this. You go see your dad. I'll take the SUV back to Shane so he can come back for you."

Banks nodded. "Thanks. I really appreciate everything."

Axton gave him a one-arm hug and then motioned for Adan to follow. "Come on."

Adan grabbed his bag and scrambled to his feet. He didn't question Axton at all. Banks had no idea what Axton planned to do with the guy. Honestly, Banks wasn't sure if he cared. He was just numb.

Kyson linked fingers with him, and they headed inside. They paused at the entryway. The place was completely trashed. Antiques were smashed on the floor. Paintings were ripped from the walls. The armed guards, who always looked stoic and invisible, were very visibly skittish and ready to bolt. A few were obviously upset. Banks stepped his way through the mess while keeping Kyson safe from the glass. They finally found everyone inside the family sitting room. Everything was destroyed there too. His dad sat in the middle of the couch with an open bottle of whiskey on his knee. It was almost empty. He looked worse than Banks had ever seen him.

Banks stared at him.

Beau didn't acknowledge them at all. He simply stared at nothing. Blood dripped from his busted knuckles.

Each breath Banks took came harder than the last. His father had done this. He had killed their mother. Maybe he never laid a hand on her, but he still murdered her every bit as much as pulling the trigger.

"I just wanted her to choose me. I just wanted her to put down the bottle and choose us."

At Beau's dead-sounding words, the truth washed over him. Adan. Every terrible thing his father had done right in his mother's face. All of it had been an angry, bitter man's desperate and fury-filled struggle to get their mom to fight.

The demon burst from Banks. "You mother—" He launched himself at Beau with all the fury he possessed. Boone snatched him from his feet before he landed a single blow. All Banks saw was red. He struggled with everything he had had as Boone strong-armed him from the room. Boone spoke, but Banks couldn't hear a thing. His only goal was murder. Unfortunately, even at the height of his rage, Boone was bigger and stronger than him.

"Stop, baby." Kyson's words were the only thing that penetrated the pounding in his ears.

Boone half walked, half carried Banks into the conversation room. It was where the family always sat with guests, while the dining room table was set, so everyone could have a drink beforehand. It was also where everyone gathered afterward to eat their dessert and have another drink. Their mom's life did revolve around alcohol.

Banks blinked, and Kyson was in front of him.

He held Banks' face between his hands. "Just breathe. Focus on me. Breathe."

Banks held his stare. Kyson's beautiful green eyes had him going still in Boone's hold.

"That's it, baby." He inhaled. "Inhale."

Banks followed his lead and inhaled.

"Good. Keep breathing."

With Kyson as his sole focus, his heart rate slowly dropped.

Boone's hold on him relaxed. "Are you good?"

Kyson nodded. "Go. We'll be fine."

Boone released Banks and left them alone.

Kyson never looked away from him. "I know you're hurting. Let me take care of you. Tearing someone to shreds won't help. Fall on me instead. I have you."

Banks nodded. He had no idea what he agreed to, but he needed something to take away the pain. Banks knew Kyson would do his damnedest.

"Okay." Kyson took his hand and headed for the stairs. He didn't stop until they were inside Banks' childhood bedroom. Kyson closed the door behind them. He locked the door. "Come on." Kyson led him to bed before working on stripping away his clothes. Once he had Banks down to his underwear, he pulled back the covers. "Get in."

Banks did as told. He swore his mind had snapped or fled. Banks no longer knew anything except that he loved Kyson and he hurt. All he could do was trust Kyson to fix it.

Kyson's heart was completely shattered. He had loved Tabitha. She had warned him, and he hadn't truly heard her. Not that he could have stopped her. Kyson couldn't stop anything bad from happening. He never had. Oddly, Kyson still felt calmer than he had in ages. In control. He loved Banks. Banks needed him. This was something he could do. Maybe he wasn't good for much. But when it came to loving Banks, he was an expert.

After stripping down to his underwear, Kyson climbed into bed next to Banks and held him as tightly as he could. It was late.

There was nothing they could do tonight. Banks needed to be held and comforted. He needed sleep. Kyson would ensure he had everything it required to survive this.

"Would you like me to find you a drink or one of your cigars? I'm sure there's something like that around here. Whatever you need, I'm on it. However I can help, in any way, I will."

"I chose you." Banks' voice broke.

It took Kyson a second, but the truth dawned. Unlike his mom, Banks chose love. His throat swelled. Then he made the mistake of meeting Banks' stare. A tear slipped from Banks' eye. Like that, Kyson broke. His body jerked as the first cry hit. Kyson cried so hard, he thought he might puke. Even though Banks had tears spilling from his eyes, he still held Kyson and comforted him. They were each other's rock. It was the first real, gut-wrenching cry Kyson had let himself fall into since Jack. He had been scared if he fell apart, he would never be whole again. But Banks and he had each other. They would face tomorrow together.

Banks kissed his cheek. "*Shhh*, baby. I'm here. She loved you so much."

It broke his heart even more that Banks felt like he needed to comfort him. He didn't know how to explain how the floodgates had simply opened. Tabitha's death was just the final straw.

Banks sat up and stacked the pillows against the headboard before leaning against them. "Okay. Come here, baby."

Kyson dutifully straddled Banks' lap and buried his face in the crook of his neck.

Banks pulled the covers up and tucked them around Kyson. He rubbed Kyson's back. "I don't think I can handle setting eyes on Dad for a while. Sometimes, I scare myself with how far I'll go. I think we should go away for a little while." He kissed Kyson's forehead. "Not forever. I know you have a family and Soren is here. Obviously, I have my brother. But I think we need a break from—I don't know—the vibes, I guess."

Kyson lightly sucked Banks' neck to soothe himself. He understood what Banks meant. So much bad had happened, and even though they had found each other amongst the rubble, the bad still lingered like a cloud.

"When we were kids, Mom used to take us to Colorado to go skiing. We stayed at this ritzy-ass resort, of course. By no means did Mom ever rough it. But we would ski the bunny slope and then sit by the fire and drink hot chocolate. Those are some of the few times I remember feeling like this was a normal family. It took me a long time to real- ize Mom sliced those normal moments out of life for us. She made sure we understood peace and happiness. If there is any good in me, it came from her."

Kyson thought Banks was ninety percent his mother. He had the best heart.

"I'd love to do that again. It's not the same, obviously. But I want to slice some normal moments out of life for us. I want to marry you and always have a peaceful place to fall." He took a shaky-sounding breath. "I swear I'd never fail you the way my family failed me. The way we've failed each other."

Kyson sniffed. "You're incapable of failing me. I want all those things too."

Banks' arms tightened around him. "I love you."

Kyson kissed Banks' neck. "I love you too."

"Let's get some sleep."

Kyson nodded. Tomorrow would likely be a long and horrible day. If Kyson knew nothing else, he knew they needed their strength. There was no telling what hell awaited them with the sun, and grief was never ending.

CHAPTER EIGHT

BANKS DRAGGED A HALF-ASLEEP Kyson from bed at the ungodly hour of four a.m. to leave for Colorado. Kyson had tried arguing he would regret not going to his mother's funeral. Banks knew his mother would want no one to see her like that. She was gone. Banks needed to deal with it his way.

He had spoken to Boone before waking Kyson. Banks hadn't wanted to disappoint his brother. Together, they had decided it would be best if Banks left. He couldn't promise he wouldn't find his hands around his father's throat. Banks absolutely did not want to end up at the bottom of a bottle of alcohol or pills. He had to walk away from this before he lost the will to be sober for Kyson.

The moment they were in the air, Banks had gone a step further and blocked his dad's number. He doubted the move would be permanent, but Banks wasn't sure about anything at the moment. Kyson held his hand. They didn't talk much. Once they settled into the ski resort, they went straight back to bed. Life just felt too exhausting. While Kyson slept, Banks stared at the ceiling. His skin itched and his mind raced. He had to force his mind away from his mom. Banks grabbed his phone and searched for jewelers in the area. He didn't mind paying exorbitant fees as long as they delivered and did so fast. From there, Banks researched getting married where they were. He wanted this now, but he also needed it to be beautiful for Kyson. Thankfully, it looked like he had options. Kyson felt like the only family he had at the moment. He needed to solidify that and ensure Kyson had the protection of his last name. Banks needed something to keep his focus.

With a plan in place, Banks set his phone aside and stared at Kyson. Kyson wore the adorable bat pajamas Banks loved so much. He hadn't worn them since the day he came to live with Banks. Banks supposed his confession about that day had taken the trauma away from Kyson wearing the outfit. At least, he hoped it had. Kyson was the first person in the world to make him feel like he didn't break everything he touched.

Kyson rolled. He smiled when he saw Banks awake. "Why aren't you sleeping?"

"My mind won't stop racing."

Kyson stroked his chest. "What can I do?"

Banks shrugged. "I'm the daddy. I do the soothing."

A sweet smile touched Kyson's lips. "Maybe we can take turns sometimes. When you had a daddy—not trying to trigger you—what did he do to help you sleep?"

Banks' throat nearly swelled closed. "How did you know I had a daddy?" He never wanted Kyson to see him as weak. Banks hated remembering exactly how much power he had handed to someone who didn't deserve it. His need for love had nearly killed him.

A line appeared between Kyson's eyebrows. "You told me. That night when I sat with you on the bathroom floor. You told me about him. I'm sorry. It never occurred to me you didn't remember, or that you didn't want me to know." He looked truly upset.

Banks kissed his forehead. "Don't worry about it. It's just a part of my life I try really hard to forget." He shrugged. "It's just..."

"Humiliating," Kyson supplied for him. "I know." He took a deep breath. "I'm struggling to hang on to the joy I used to feel being a Little. For a while now, every time I walk into The PlayPen, I feel like everyone looks at me and sees me as a weak idiot. I've never been so embarrassed to be me as I have been since Jack. But I also don't know how to make people understand. Anyone crazy enough to do the things Jack did is crazy enough to kill you. To the bottom of my soul, I knew one day he would do just that and it would come sooner rather than later if I left. I'm sorry. I shouldn't have brought up your past. You gave up that side of yourself to survive. I understand."

Kyson broke his heart but also made him so fucking proud. He felt safe enough to say all those words to Banks. Banks wasn't failing him. "No. You're allowed to talk to me about anything at all. It's my job to listen, comfort you, and love you. I know I also have all those things in you." Banks took a breath. This conversation freed his brain from the hell it had been suffering. Banks would take a conversation about the past over current circumstances. "Shutting down that side of myself isn't how I coped. I opened The PlayPen. Back when it was me, I didn't have anywhere safe to go. Maybe if I had, someone could've helped me before I killed him."

"It was him or you."

Banks nodded. "It was, but I also recognize how much I simply let happen to me. Being raised by wolves fucked me up. I wanted to feel some innocence and love so fucking badly, I was willing to do anything. Then one day, something else roared to life inside me.

A monster I can't always control. Maybe he fucked something up in my head. I don't know. All I know is, I'm not the same." Banks blinked. He hadn't realized how far he had fallen into his thoughts until he realized he didn't even see Kyson in front of him. Banks focused on Kyson. He cleared his throat. "Anyhow, that's how I ended up owning a very particular fetish club."

Kyson's beautiful green eyes moved over Banks' face. "I wish you saw how absolutely amazing you are. You're one of the best people I've ever met in my life, and you don't even know it."

Banks laughed. There was no humor in the sound. "Baby, love makes you blind. You're overlooking who I am. No matter what happens when the dust settles, I'll always be Banks Bosi. I'll always be the son of Beau Bosi. There will never come a day when I can walk away from that. When you marry me, it'll be the same for you."

Kyson stroked his cheek. "I fell in love with Banks Bosi, son of Beau Bosi, and I have zero regrets. Bring on the wedding."

A smile exploded across Banks' face. "Funny you should say that."

Kyson's eyebrows rose and a smile that felt evil stretched Banks' lips. His mom had adored Kyson. He knew nothing in the world would've made her happier than knowing Banks had married him. There was no better way to honor her. Plus, he was just sickeningly in love. It was a win win.

Kyson couldn't say how he went from seeing his first massive pile of snow to getting married. Both were beautiful. There was a hint of sadness, knowing none of their friends or family were there. The devastation of knowing Tabitha was gone still lingered just out of sight the entire time. But Banks needed this marriage to happen exactly when it did. Kyson imagined it was the only thing saving his sanity. He would do absolutely anything for Banks.

Somehow Banks had gotten them rings and a cake. The ring was a little big, and the cake was dry, but Kyson still loved every detail.

"Boop." Banks bumped a bit of cake against Kyson's lips and then came in to lick it away.

Kyson couldn't stop smiling. "Was that your version of smashing cake in my face?"

Banks wore a huge grin. "Yeah, well. No one hits you in the face. Not even me. Not even playfully."

Kyson's forehead furrowed. "You mean like this?" He smeared a handful of cake across Banks' cheek. Kyson had been working on digging his fingers into the cake on the sly for a minute.

Banks roared with laughter.

The sound was music to Kyson's ears. He had done that. In the midst of a nightmare, Kyson had still given Banks a beautiful moment. Maybe he hadn't completely lost the childlike part of himself. Kyson wiped his fingers on a napkin while Banks tried wiping the cake from his face. He missed most of it.

"Here." Kyson took the napkin from him and cleaned his face. It was odd to be having such a moment with a photographer taking nonstop photos. Then again, he kept forgetting she was there. Like almost always, it was just them in their bubble. The way it had been since Kyson came to live with Banks. They had insulated themselves, found peace, and did some healing together. They had fallen in love so quietly, it had been almost natural—like they had always been meant to be together. There hadn't been a grand moment of realization. It was more of a slow acceptance of the truth. This was a quiet, peaceful love. Perfect in every way.

Banks stared at Kyson with so much adoration, it swelled Kyson's throat. "Thank you."

Kyson stopped wiping his face to focus on Banks. "For what?"

"For loving me. Marrying me. For your faith."

A lump grew in Kyson's throat. "Same."

Banks lowered his head.

Kyson met him halfway. Everything inside Kyson melted as their tongues brushed.

"We'll box up this cake for you."

Banks pulled away and kissed Kyson's forehead before focusing on the woman in charge of the wedding chapel. "Thank you. We appreciate how quickly you pulled this together."

A bright smile lit her face. "Of course."

Banks focused on him again. "Are you ready to go start our life together as husbands?"

Kyson's face hurt from smiling. "Absolutely." He knew the grief would be back to slap them soon enough. But for now, they were carving their piece of happiness from life—just the way Tabitha would have wanted.

CHAPTER NINE

WHILE KYSON HELD A bouquet of roses in one hand and a box of cake in the other, Banks carried him over the threshold of their room. Kyson couldn't stop smiling. Banks had changed his life so much. It was immeasurable, honestly. Kyson set his haul on the first flat surface they passed on the way to bed. Banks went quiet on the trek. Kyson's heart squeezed. He worried the rush of the day had worn off and now Banks regretted his rash decision. Kyson couldn't take it.

"Regretting me already, huh?"

Banks blinked and glanced down at Kyson. "Of course not. Why would you say that?"

Kyson shrugged as Banks set him on the edge of the bed. "Your dark expression."

After dropping to his knees, Banks went to work undressing Kyson. "Sorry. My brain is all over the place. It's definitely not you." He removed Kyson's shirt. "You have my full attention now."

A sad smile pulled at the corners of Kyson's mouth. "It's okay. We can just cuddle. I know this wasn't..." Kyson didn't know what he intended to say. It wasn't a typical wedding. This likely wasn't what Banks really wanted. This wasn't about him. He didn't know anymore.

Banks' gaze moved over Kyson's face. He stood and toppled Kyson onto his back before straddling him. Banks kept his weight on his knees so he didn't squish Kyson. His expression kept Kyson frozen. He looked enraged. "This wasn't what?"

Kyson had never been scared of Banks. He feared he was headed that way now. Kyson shrugged. His gaze slid away. "Forget I said anything." Even Kyson heard how small and frightened he sounded.

Banks touched Kyson's jaw, forcing him to meet Banks' stare. His voice and eyes softened. "No. Please tell me. If this wasn't what you wanted, you can say that. I would never hurt you."

Kyson's muscles relaxed. He knew that. Sometimes trauma got the best of him. "I've never wanted anything more than I want you. I'm just worried you'll wake up in few weeks or months and realize you did this out of grief." Kyson shook his head. "It would kill me if you regretted us."

Banks' serious expression never wavered. That fact lent power to his words. "You have to let go of this idea I could ever regret you. I don't think you understand how much you should've never looked my way. You should've never given trash like me a chance." Banks braced his palms on either side of Kyson's head and went nose to nose with him. "But you did and now you're mine. I'll never let you get away. You're exactly what I've always wanted. There's no going back or escape for you. There sure as fuck will be no regrets. On either side," Banks said, sounding firm—like it was an order, not a reassurance.

"Then you should definitely make love to me."

Kyson barely got the words out before Banks' mouth covered his. His tongue moved lazily, teasing Kyson. Kyson moaned as Banks' mouth moved from Kyson's lips to his throat. He adored the way Banks sucked his skin. Before Banks, he hadn't realized how arousing it was to feel a tongue stroking his neck. He squirmed as his cock hardened. His skin itched. He needed Banks to fix it.

Banks moved lower, biting and sucking his way down Kyson's body. He unbuttoned Kyson's pants along the way. Kyson whimpered when his dick was in Banks' hand. He didn't know long he would survive this torture. Then Banks swallowed his cock. Kyson's body nearly jackknifed from the bed. A sound escaped him he had never made. Once when he was a teen, and experimenting with a friend, they had sucked each other. Since then, no one had ever sucked his dick. It was a duty expected of him as a Little. He couldn't stop moving against Banks' mouth. Kyson knew he would die if Banks stopped.

Much faster than Kyson wanted, the familiar pressure of an oncoming orgasm climbed his shaft. Mewling sounds came from the back of his throat. Banks didn't slow. He pleasured Kyson like he loved it. Kyson's mind was a mess. He babbled his love. His sanity was on the edge as saliva ran down his balls. His muscles tensed. Kyson held his breath and strained toward the release. He blew. A whining struggle for air came out in pants as Banks sucked him dry. Kyson still hadn't caught his breath by the time Banks mouth covered his again.

Suddenly, Banks sprang from the bed. Cold air blasted Kyson's nude body. He barely had time to recover his wits before Banks' naked skin molded to his. Banks didn't hesitate to shove a slippery cock inside him. The moment he was buried to the hilt, Banks stopped. He worshipped Kyson's mouth while his dick simply warmed itself inside Kyson's ass.

Kyson felt restless again. He had never gone soft and the sensation of Banks' cock stretching him wide had his skin tingling again.

Banks' mouth moved from Kyson's lips to his ear. He did the tiniest of hip rolls, massaging that internal button that got Kyson hot. "Show Daddy how you can come just from his dick. Let me feel that tight little asshole sucking me dry." He barely rocked inside Kyson, keeping the perfect pressure. Kyson thought his sanity might snap. "Be a good boy. Make Daddy's cock spit. You know how good that makes me feel."

Holy shit. He wasn't going to survive. Kyson hadn't wanted this play in so long. Banks was pulling all the kinks from him. He whimpered.

"That's right, sweet angel. You can do it. It's so cute when you squirm beneath me. You know I always make you feel good."

Kyson scratched at his skin. He needed more, but he also didn't want Banks to stop playing. "Please, Daddy. It's doing that thing where I need to touch it."

"You won't."

"But I like it when the liquid comes out."

Banks pumped inside him. "Then make that happen to Daddy's hard-on. He likes it too."

Kyson exploded into action. He didn't recall how it happened, but he had Banks on his back. Kyson took what he wanted. He rode Banks' dick the way he liked. With his head thrown back and sucking air, Kyson used Banks. He ground down on Banks' cock. Insanity ruled him. Kyson wound tighter by the second. Banks talked, but Kyson didn't hear a word. His every fiber was focused on blowing cum on Banks' skin. The pleasure grew bigger and bigger until it exploded into ecstasy.

Kyson cried out over and over as he rode out each wave. He heard Banks shout, but it was a muted thing. His orgasm was all that mattered. When he collapsed onto Banks' chest, he didn't care about the mess. Kyson's muscles simply melted. His energy zapped. He didn't know what tomorrow would bring. But right now, Kyson was on top of the world with his husband. Nothing could touch them here.

Again, Banks watched Kyson sleep. It was nearing dinnertime. He knew he would need to wake Kyson soon. For now, he just needed this. Kyson brought him so much peace. It was almost funny. He had always believed he would struggle hard if he ever stayed sober. Maybe he had done so many different drugs over the years, his body didn't know what to miss. Maybe he was just numb outside of anything that wasn't Kyson. Whatever the reason, he was strangely fine. He couldn't disappoint Kyson. He couldn't lose Kyson. Those two fears were bigger than any high. Maybe that was the crux of things. Before Kyson, he didn't have a reason to live. He had just been racing to the grave—just like his mom. That thought was terrifying, because—just like his mom—if Kyson chose to break him, there would be no going back. Things were just too hard without him.

A light knock had Banks' gaze shooting toward the door. It came again. Banks eyed Kyson. He slept soundly. Banks slipped from the bed, found a pair of pajama pants, and headed for the door. He closed the door between the bedroom and living room to keep from disturbing Kyson. Banks checked the peephole. Boone and Jupiter stood on the other side.

Banks tried flattening his hair as he opened the door. "Hey, guys. What's up?" He knew he had to look as confused as he felt, but he immediately stepped aside to let the pair inside.

Boone headed for the couch.

Jupiter followed in his wake.

Boone didn't respond until they were seated. "Dad is trying to make Mom's funeral a damn carnival. You know how much she would've hated that. So, Jupiter and I talked about it, and you're right. The best way we can honor her is being here—together. This was her favorite place, and this is where she was always the happiest. Are you wearing a wedding ring?"

The sudden pivot in conversation had Banks slow to react. "Uh. Yeah. Kyson and I got married."

Jupiter smiled. "Yay! Congratulations."

Boone looked hurt. "You got married without me?"

Banks sat on the loveseat across from them. He picked up a throw pillow and hugged it to his chest. Banks didn't know how to explain how much he needed to tie Kyson to him to save his life and sanity. He had to know the only other person who loved him as much as his mother had wasn't going to leave him too.

"I'm happy for you," Boone said before Banks could find the words. "Kyson has been good for you. I've never seen you sober this long."

Banks nodded. "I don't know how to do this life without him." He didn't know where the confession came from, but his voice broke. His vision swam. Grief kept hitting him when he least expected. Then Kyson was there. He was a furry bat again.

Kyson swiped at his cheeks. "It's okay, baby. I'm right here."

Banks focused on his beautiful green eyes until he could breathe again.

A sweet smile touched Kyson's lips. "There you go. Just breathe."

When he sucked in a ragged breath, the room looked a bit clearer. He found Boone starting a fire in the fireplace and Jupiter inspecting their cake. It was obvious they had found something to do, so he didn't feel watched.

Banks took another breath. He cleared his throat. "You two should grab your things and crash here. There's three bedrooms. You can join us in your pjs, and we can order room service."

Boone looked his way, smiling. "Just like we used to do with Mom."

Banks nodded. "Exactly. We can get a store delivery of marshmallows and whatnot to make s'mores."

"Oh, God. We used to make such a mess."

A chuckle slipped from Banks at Boone's remark. "Mom would make us take a bath and then we'd just get right back into the candy. We drove her so crazy."

"She never lost her temper."

They shared a smile. This was right. They were meant to celebrate her here. Banks took a breath. She was finally at peace. No more pain. He wanted that for her. Banks just wished it didn't hurt quite so much.

CHAPTER TEN

WITH HIS BACK LEANED against Banks' chest, Kyson eyed the room. The PlayPen seemed unusually busy today. Boone sat on the floor across from them, holding Jupiter. Soren played with his cars while patiently waiting for his turn to play their board game with Luca. Jarek sat at a table with Beau, going over some paperwork. Boone and Banks were doing their obvious best to ignore him. Kyson couldn't stop looking at everyone, including Adan. Adan sat alone with his back to the room. The hood of his bunny pajamas hid his face. He played with a racetrack and ignored everyone.

Jupiter followed his line of gaze. He curled his nose. "He has a lot of nerve being here."

Kyson felt Banks shrug. "I built this place as a haven for all Littles, even him. Does your guy have glasses?"

Jupiter looked at his Guess Who board. "No."

Kyson closed the tabs that had characters with glasses. "If it would make you more comfortable, we could go to our place instead."

Jupiter didn't respond right away. He looked Boone's way. There was a deep line between Boone's eyebrows. "Nah. It's fine. Banks is right. Plus, it looks like my baby is working on a headache. We should go before it gets worse."

They passed their boards to Soren and Luca before giving hugs. The moment the pair left, Kyson snuggled deeper into Banks' hold. Banks hadn't said a word, but Kyson worried about Beau being there. So far, Beau hadn't tried talking to him. He feared the silence would end the moment his meeting with Jarek did.

"What's your plan?"

Banks didn't play dumb. "I don't know."

"What do you need right now?"

Banks' arms tightened around him.

Kyson couldn't help but smile. Before Banks, he had felt so small and useless. With him, Kyson was strong and had a purpose. "I've been thinking."

Banks kissed the shell of his ear. "About?"

Kyson shrugged. "Maybe we didn't stay gone long enough. I mean, there're lots of other places I've never seen."

He felt Banks smile against his ear. "Maybe we should do that."

Beau stood.

Kyson held his breath.

He headed for the door without looking their way. Kyson didn't know if that was worse. It was possible, eventually, Banks might feel like he lost both his parents. It was possible he already felt that way. It was equally possible he had.

Jarek crossed the room and joined them. He held out a stack of papers. "Your mom's estate."

Banks didn't reach for them. "Thank you." He simply held Kyson tighter.

Kyson accepted on his behalf. To his surprise, on top, there was an envelope for him. He shot Jarek a questioning look. "What's this?"

A sad smile touched Jarek's lips. "Something Tabitha asked me to give to you."

Kyson plucked the envelope from the paper clip. He was too curious to have a modicum of patience. Under the envelope was a check to Banks for an ungodly amount. Kyson set the papers on his lap and opened the envelope. He unfolded the pages inside.

Kyson,

I told you there was only one way out.

Tears immediately filled Kyson's eyes. He had to look away to compose himself before reading farther.

It won't be the same for you. Banks will choose you and you'll be happy until the day you pass away holding hands.

Kyson's heart squeezed as the meaning of her words sank in. The next lines confirmed his thoughts.

Yes, I've always known what Beau is playing at, but still. Whether he ever admits it to himself or not, he does love Adan. He wouldn't have kept up this act for ten long years if he didn't. Oh, God, they've been so long. My life has been such a wild swing from addiction to wanting to stop for Beau, to needing the escape from Beau. Then the kids grew up, and it was just us. The three of us.

Kyson practically felt her hatred and sadness in that one sentence.

Still, I hung on for Boone and Banks' sake as long as I could. But I know they're going to be okay without me. I told you Banks has a little too much of me inside him. Maybe that's true, but he's also nothing like me. He'll be strong for you. He looks at you with so much love. You have no idea how much I love you for that alone.

Kyson swiped at his eyes. He had to keep reading.

Even without that, though, I love you so very much. Thank you for all the times you saw me, sat with me, and did your damnedest to bring me comfort. But, baby, there just isn't enough handholding or alcohol in the world to fix what broke in me. Please keep my baby safe. I know he'll marry you the second he thinks he can convince you, so I asked Jarek to give you this after your wedding. I'll be gone before then and I'm sorry for that. This is the only comfort I can give you in return. Please use it to give

Banks a normal life. Please help him make some happy memories.

I will love you always,

Tabitha

Kyson moved to the next page. It was a check with several zeros. The next page was a deed to a cabin in Colorado. Kyson couldn't keep his tears at bay or silent any longer. Banks kept one arm wrapped around him while Kyson fell apart and while reading the letter. After a moment, Banks' hand simply dropped to Kyson's lap, still holding the note.

Jarek cleared his throat. "There's a letter for you too, Banks. Unfortunately, it was at the house at the time of her death. I have to wait until the police release it."

"It's fine." Banks sounded oddly okay. "She gave me the world already. I have my closure." He kissed Kyson's shoulder.

Jarek nodded. "She was an amazing lady. I'm so sorry for your loss."

Kyson swiped at his eyes again. He took a shaky breath. Tabitha was right. Banks was so damn strong. Kyson was proud as hell of being his husband. He looked at the deed again. "Leave it to your mom to have impeccable timing. It seems we're not done traveling."

He felt Banks smile against his cheek. "Maybe Soren and Shane would like to go with us this time."

Soren looked up from his game board, blinking. "What? Where am I going with Shane?"

A smile exploded across Kyson's face. They would have a good life together. It was time to look toward the future. He was excited to see this cabin and even more thrilled at the idea of torturing Shane by thrusting Soren into his path. The giant had an unmistakable glint in his eye when he looked at Soren. It was time to foster some happiness and leave the past behind.

Keep an eye out for the next Little Lost, *In Daddy's Care*.

About the Author

CHARITY PARKERSON IS AN award-winning and multi-published author with several companies. Born with no filter from her brain to her mouth, she decided to take this odd quirk and insert it in her characters. One of her greatest loves is writing morally gray characters. You'll find them scattered throughout her hundreds of titles.

*Eight-time Readers' Favorite Award Winner

*2015 Passionate Plume Award Finalist

*2013 Reviewers' Choice Award Winner

*2012 ARRA Finalist for Favorite Paranormal Romance

*Five-time winner of The Mistress of the Darkpath

Connect with her online:

*Sign up for her newsletter: https://bit.ly/charityparkersonnewsletter

*Join her readers' group on Facebook: http://bit.ly/CharitysTribe

*Website: https://www.charityparkerson.com

*A list of her social media accounts and giveaways all in one place: http://hy.page/charityparkerson

www.ingramcontent.com/pod-product-compliance
Lightning Source LLC
Chambersburg PA
CBHW070934250626
47159CB00009B/3244